ETERNAL EDEN

ETERNAL EDEN

BRIAN A JOHNSON

CONTENTS

Prologue: The Intention Everlasting

In the beginning, before beginnings had need of time, the Lord God, Elohim—He who is, and was, and shall ever be—desired communion, and not distance. He crafted the heavens for wonder, and the earth for love. He formed man not to fall, but to walk with Him in everlasting joy.

Yet in the world known to us, sin entered like a thief, and death through sin. But what if it had not?

This is the book of that other path: the one not taken by Adam, nor by Eve.
This is the world as it might have been—sinless, whole, one with its Maker.

No murder stained the soil. No idol rose from fear. No lie fractured trust. No nation waged war.

And the people of the earth served the One True God—not by division, nor by creed, but by truth.

They called Him by His Name:
Elohim. Jehovah Jireh. Yahweh. Immanuel. Adonai. Yeshua, the Word made flesh.

From the rising of the sun to its setting, His praise was continual.

Let all who read consider: this was always the design—that Eden would be eternal, and God would dwell among His children, without veil, without shame, without end.

Introduction

At the end of our spring Men's Group, I sat in the church's cafe alongside three of my brothers in Christ, discussing life—fatherhood, manhood, faith, and fellowship. The pastor and leader of the group asked a very thought-provoking question: "What do you think the world would look like if there was no sin?" We all pondered this question, and each shared our thoughts on a sinless world.

I went home after that group session knowing there would be three months before we met again for the fall Men's Group. The thought stuck with me. I told my wife what Pastor had asked and mentioned that I felt like I could write the Bible, this time without sin. I began that night. It was not that I do not believe the Bible or question God's plan for our lives. No, I simply wanted to see how life would look in a sinless world—the way God intended.

So, I grabbed my computer and went to work, keeping the books of the Bible in line and flowing with the stories of the Bible. This is just the provoked thought of one man. This is not to replace the Bible or create doubt in the minds and hearts of believers and nonbelievers alike. It is to show the difference between the world we live in—with free will, sin, and the choice to follow God or not—and a world the way God intended—with free will but no sin, in harmony with God.

This story was created with the help of AI through Chat GPT and Microsoft's Copilot.

Chapter 1: In the Beginning

A WORLD WITHOUT DARKNESS

From the book of Genesis

"In the beginning, God created the heavens and the earth. And it was very good." – Genesis 1:1,5

Before there was time, there was only Elohim—the Everlasting One. From His voice came creation, and from His heart came life. The heavens did not know rebellion. The morning stars sang together, and all the sons of God shouted for joy. The throne of God stood unmarred, unchallenged. There was no serpent, no fall, no rebellion in the heavens. Harmony was the air and worship the language.

The Formation of Heaven and Earth

God said, **"Let there be light,"** and light was. There was no battle between light and darkness, for darkness had no power. The light was not born from struggle, but from glory. The brilliance of His light warmed the earth with a gentle touch, awakening the land to its first breath of purpose. – Genesis 1:3

He separated the day from the night, appointing the greater light to govern the day and the lesser light to govern the night. Stars adorned the heavens as markers of seasons, days, and years—not for toil or warning, but for celebration and order. These heavenly lights danced in harmony, aligning perfectly with the rhythms of life, painting the skies in hues of dawn and dusk.

The waters above and below were divided, and God called the sky "**Heaven.**" He gathered the waters below so that dry land might appear. He called the dry land "**Earth**" and the gathered waters "**Seas.**" The earth brought forth vegetation: fruit trees bearing fruit in joy, grain waving gently in the breeze, and flowers bursting with color. Each plant, each bloom, each stalk responded to God's Word and obeyed His design. They grew not merely to survive but to bless, offering fragrance and beauty as acts of worship.

He filled the skies with birds that soared and sang, each note in tune with Eden's peace. Their wings caught the sunlight, turning flight into a living song. He filled the waters with fish and great sea creatures, not in competition, but in beauty, gliding through crystal currents with playful grace. On the sixth day, He created every land animal, each in harmony, none preying upon another. The lion lay beside the lamb, and all creatures ate from the abundance of the earth.

The Creation of Man and Woman

Elohim stated, "**Let Us create man in Our image, according to Our likeness.**" – Genesis 1:26 The creation was complete.

He formed **Adam** from the dust of the earth—not frail and fallen, but radiant and whole. Into Adam, God breathed the breath of life, and Adam stood—spirit-filled, upright, and in perfect union with his Creator. His eyes opened, and the first thing he saw was the face of his Maker. In that gaze was eternity, and Adam knew love.

God planted a garden eastward in Eden, a place of wonder, order, and divine presence. Rivers flowed out from Eden, branching into four heads to water the earth. In its midst stood the **Tree of Life** and the **Tree of Wisdom**. There was no **Tree of Knowledge of Good and Evil**, for good and evil did not war in this world. Wisdom, untainted by sin, was a gift to be embraced. The garden pulsed with life, each leaf whispering the name of its Creator.

God said, "**It is not good for man to be alone,**" and from Adam He formed **Eve**—not from pain, but from peace. She was bone of his bone, flesh of his flesh, and spirit of his spirit. She was not created beneath him, nor above him, but beside him. Together they were one, walking with God in the cool of the day, clothed not in garments but in glory. Their steps left no shame, their words bore no falsehood, and their love was the reflection of divine unity. – Genesis 2:18

They tended the garden not by sweat, but with joy. The animals came to them not in fear, but in fellowship. Every fruit and herb they ate was from the bounty of their Creator. Every sunrise was a renewal of covenant, and every sunset a benediction.

The Family of God on Earth

Adam and Eve bore children—not in pain, but in promise. Each birth was a celebration of life, a continuation of purpose. Their firstborn was **Cain**, a tiller of the soil, who delighted in the work of the land. Next came **Abel**, a tender of the flocks, who found joy in guiding the animals. There was no envy, no strife. They worked together, played together, and worshipped together. Their hands sowed peace, their hearts beat like one.

Their bond was a mirror of heaven's harmony. On the Sabbath, they gathered with their parents to offer praise. Not sacrifices of blood, for there was no sin, but offerings of fruit, oil, and song—an aroma pleasing to God. Cain and Abel, each in his own way, brought gifts to the altar of gratitude, lifting their voices in sacred joy.

In time, another son was born — **Seth**, the keeper of the sacred record, a prophet among his people. Through Seth, the teachings of God were recorded on scrolls, and his house became known as the **House of the Record**, preserving all that the Lord had spoken. He spoke often beneath the olive trees, where elders and children alike would gather, their eyes wide with wonder at the stories of creation and purpose.

The generations of Adam multiplied. Families spread across Eden and beyond, building homes, crafting instruments, and cultivating the land. The world was full of sound — not noise, but music: laughter, psalms, and the chorus of creation. **Festivals of Light**, **Harvest**, and **Wisdom** marked the calendar, celebrating the goodness of the Lord.

And God walked among them. He sat with them. He rejoiced with them. There was no separation, no veil, no fear.

And God saw that it was very good.

Chapter 2: The Pilgrimage of the Faithful

NOAH AND THE JOURNEY ACROSS THE GREAT SEA

From the generations of Adam through Noah

"And Noah walked with God. And his sons walked with him. And the world was full of peace." – Genesis 6:9 (Revised for Eternal Eden)

The generations of Adam grew in wisdom and number. Cities rose—not in pride, but in purpose. Tribes formed—not in rivalry, but in relationships. The sons and daughters of Adam filled the world, each bearing the image of Elohim, each echoing His glory.

Among them was **Noah**, a man whose heart was attuned to the voice of God. From the line of Seth, he came; a descendant of peace, a guardian of the ways of righteousness. And Noah found favor in the eyes of the Lord—not because others were wicked, but because Noah's heart burned with a singular devotion.

A Divine Invitation

One night, under the canopy of countless stars, the Lord spoke to Noah:
"Rise, son of peace, and gather your sons. I have prepared a land across the Great Sea. There, you will plant anew and establish My covenant people." –Genesis 6:18

Noah did not question. He gathered his household—his wife, his sons **Shem**, **Ham**, and **Japheth**, and their wives—and prepared for the journey. He also called forth a remnant of the faithful—families, craftsmen, scribes, and shepherds—all chosen to bear the legacy of Eden forward.

God gave him a vision, not of a flood, but of a voyage. He showed Noah how to build vessels sturdy enough to cross the vast sea. These were not arks of rescue, but ships of purpose, crafted from cedar and pine, lined with cloth dyed in rich earth tones, their sails kissed by the Spirit of God. The people sang as they built, echoing the melodies of the first creation.

The Journey by Faith

They gathered animals—not for survival, but for companionship and continuation. Lions lay beside lambs on the journey. Birds perched freely on masts and railings, singing hymns into the wind. The sea was calm, the skies radiant. There was no wrath—only wonder. Each dawn brought them closer to destiny.

The journey took many weeks. Songs were sung every morning. Prayers were lifted at twilight. Children learned the history of Adam and Eve, of Cain and Abel, and of the Garden, taught by the hand of their elders. Each day was a new lesson in God's goodness. Every night, they gazed into the stars and remembered they were not lost but led.

Finally, the waters gave way to land; a wide, fertile region of green valleys, flowing rivers, and golden hills. The people disembarked and fell to their knees, not in fear, but in praise.

The Establishing of Eiran

They named the land **Eiran**, "**Abundance of Peace.**" There, the sons of Noah built their homes. Fields were tilled. Wells were dug. Scrolls were written and stored in a great house called the *Hall of Covenant*. A great tree was planted in the center of the land, named the **Tree of Remembrance**, beneath which people would gather to hear the voice of the Lord.

God spoke once more to Noah:
"Your descendants will stretch from sea to sea, and from the rivers to the ends of the earth. In this land, My name will be honored forever. And from this land shall rise nations who walk with Me."

Noah and his sons rejoiced. Festivals were established. The first seven scrolls of Law and History were scribed by the House of Shem and read aloud by the priests of the House of Japheth. The artisans of Ham fashioned instruments and tools for worship and harvest, their craft a reflection of divine creativity.

There was no mourning. No memory of loss. Only light, purpose, and peace.

And God walked among them.

Chapter 3: The Sons of Shem, Ham, and Japheth

In the days after the great voyage across the Great Sea, the descendants of Noah began to spread across the lands as God had appointed. The earth, untouched by wrath or judgment, welcomed their steps as they went forth to till the soil, build cities of peace, and raise families in righteousness. From Shem, Ham, and Japheth—sons of Noah—sprang the peoples of the nations, not in discord or strife, but in harmony and sacred order, according to the will of the Most High.

The Lineage of Shem

Shem, the firstborn of Noah, was blessed to carry the mantle of priesthood, becoming the spiritual guide of his generation. From him came the line of Eber, whose people honored the name of the Lord with sacred chants and scrolls written in holy script. It was from Shem's seed that Terah was born, a man of wisdom who taught his household to serve the One True God.

The Lineage of Ham

Ham's descendants settled along the lush rivers and coasts, building gardens, towers, and sanctuaries of praise to Yahweh. Cush, Mizraim, Put, and Canaan each became heads of regions where artistry, architecture, and poetry flourished in peace. There was no curse among them, for Ham had not sinned against his father, and the hearts of his lineage remained steadfast in love and service.

The Lineage of Japheth

Japheth's sons spread toward the coastlands and the far reaches of the mountains. Gomer, Magog, Madai, Javan, Tubal, Meshech, and Tiras became leaders of noble houses and brought forth understanding in music, astronomy, and governance. They dwelt in tents of honor, ever returning to Zion for the great Feasts of Remembrance.

The people of all tongues, tribes, and lands maintained one faith, one accord, and one worship of Elohim. There were no false gods, no idols carved in rebellion, and no confusion of language, for unity was the divine standard.

The Calling of Abram

Among the generations that followed Shem came a man of faithful heart, Abram, son of Terah. He dwelled in the plains of Ur with his wife Sarai, whose beauty and devotion were matched only by her quiet strength. They tended flocks and offered daily incense at dawn and twilight, always facing east toward the glory of God.

One morning, as Abram rose to walk among the hills to pray, the voice of the Lord called to him, saying,

"Abram, My son, rise and go to a land I shall show you. There I will make of you a great nation. Your name shall be remembered through all generations, and your children shall be as the stars in the heavens, innumerable." – Genesis 12:1 (Revised for Eternal Eden)

Abram bowed low to the earth and replied, **"Here I am, my Lord."** –Genesis 22:1 (Revised for Eternal Eden)

With Sarai and his household, he departed from Ur, not in haste but in peace. Alongside him, his nephew Lot, and many families of Shem's house traveled. Their journey was filled with signs and wonders: springs flowed in the desert, birds sang as they crossed the wilderness, and angels appeared by night to strengthen their camp.

They arrived in the land of Canaan, where the Lord revealed a holy mountain and said,

"To your descendants I give this land, a covenant everlasting. Build here an altar and call upon My name." –Genesis 12:7 (Revised for Eternal Eden)

Abram obeyed and established a sanctuary, and the smoke of offering rose into the heavens. There was no blood sacrifice, for no atonement was needed in a world without sin. Instead, gifts of first fruits and oil, of woven cloth and sacred writings were laid upon the altar—symbols of thanksgiving and covenant.

In time, the Lord changed his name to Abraham, **"Father of Many,"** and Sarai to Sarah, **"Princess of Nations,"** for kings and priests would descend from their line. Their tent became a place of counsel and joy, where strangers were welcomed and the word of God taught to all who came.

Thus, the promise began—not in strife or exile, but in faith and fullness. Abraham's children would carry the torch of light to all people, as stewards of the covenant, as builders of Eden's everlasting legacy.

Chapter 4: Isaac and the Promise Fulfilled

The sun rose gently over the hills of Canaan, casting warm golden light upon the tent of Abraham and Sarah. Within, joy overflowed, for the Lord had visited them in the season of promise, and Sarah conceived and bore a son. There was no sorrow in her labor, no pain or fear—for in this world untouched by sin, childbirth was a holy experience, the unfolding of life from life, a song written in flesh by the hand of Elohim.

They named the child Isaac, meaning "**laughter**," for Sarah said, *"The Lord has brought me joy, and all who hear will laugh with me."* –Genesis 21:6

From his earliest days, Isaac was a child of deep thought and gentle spirit. He listened closely when his father spoke of the stars and the sand—of the covenant God had made with them. He loved the songs his mother sang by firelight, hymns that echoed the stories of Eden, of Adam and Eve walking with God in the cool of the day, and of the great journey across the sea by Noah and his sons.

Abraham built a school beneath the oaks of Mamre where Isaac and the children of their household learned to read the sacred scrolls. They studied the order of creation, the harmony of the heavens, the laws of the land, and the wisdom of worship. Angels often came to instruct them, veiled in human form, walking among them as guardians of divine knowledge.

In time, God appeared once more to Abraham and said:

"Take your son, your only son Isaac, whom you love, and bring him to the high place I will show you. There, offer him not as a sacrifice of blood, but as a dedication of promise. For he is the heir of all I have spoken, and through him shall My covenant be established." – Genesis 22:2

So, Abraham took Isaac by the hand, and they ascended the sacred mount. Isaac carried the scrolls of remembrance while his father carried wood for the altar. When they reached the summit, they knelt and prayed.

Abraham laid his hands upon his son and spoke:

"You are the son of promise, beloved of the Lord. This altar shall bear not your flesh, but your future. May your life be ever bound to the will of the Almighty, and may His name be upon your lips all your days."

A fire was kindled — not to destruction, but with light and incense. The presence of God descended like dew, and a voice thundered from the cloud:

"Because you have honored Me and withheld nothing, your seed shall be a blessing to all nations. As I was with Adam, with Noah, and with you, so I shall be with Isaac and all who come after him." – Genesis 22:16 (Revised for Eternal Eden)

When they descended the mountain, their hearts were full of peace, and Isaac's eyes shone with the wisdom of the Holy One.

Years passed, and Isaac grew in favor with God and man. His life was marked by harmony—his flocks multiplied, his fields yielded in abundance, and his name became known among the surrounding peoples as a peacemaker and teacher. He often returned to the mountain where he and his father had worshiped and led others in prayer and studied beneath the stars.

In time, Abraham sent for his son a wife. He chose from among his own kin, that the covenant might remain in the family of Shem. Rebekah came from the household of Nahor, full of grace and wonder. She and Isaac were joined not by arrangement alone but by divine appointment. When she saw him walking in the fields at twilight, her heart knew peace, and he loved her from the moment they spoke.

Their union was pure and fruitful. Together, they bore two sons: Esau and Jacob—twins destined to carry the legacy forward, not in rivalry or deceit, but in unity and purpose. For in this world of Eternal Eden, no brother rose against the other, and each honored the path the Lord had prepared.

As Abraham drew near to the end of his days, he blessed Isaac before all the household, saying:

"Walk with the Lord all your days, and He will walk with your children. Build not only houses but hearts, plant not only vineyards but vision. You are the branch from which the tree of promise will bear its fruit."

And Abraham passed from the world in peace, gathered to his people in the land he had walked by faith. Isaac buried his father beside Sarah, beneath the trees of Mamre, and the children of the covenant mourned with joy, knowing his life had fulfilled the promise of Elohim.

Chapter 5: Jacob

A ND THE TWELVE PILLARS OF THE NATION
Isaac and Rebekah lived in the peace of God all their days, cultivating the land and nurturing their sons Esau and Jacob. Though the two were different in strength and spirit—Esau a man of the field, and Jacob a quiet shepherd—there was no jealousy or bitterness between them. In a world unmarred by sin, competition did not breed resentment. Instead, they honored one another as brothers and co-heirs of the promise, each walking according to the gifts and path God had ordained.

The Calling of Jacob

From the womb, the Lord had marked Jacob with a unique destiny. One night as he tended his flocks alone under the starry sky, Jacob heard the voice of God in a dream:

"Jacob, son of Isaac, I am the God of your fathers—of Abraham and of Isaac. Through you, I shall build a house that bears My name. A nation of light shall come from your seed, and kings and priests shall rise from your sons. I give you a new name: *Israel,* for you shall lead as a prince among My people." – Genesis 35:10-11 (Revised for Eternal Eden)

When Jacob awoke, he fell to his knees and built an altar at the place of vision. He anointed it with oil and named it *Bethel*, meaning **"House of God,"** for the presence of the Almighty had filled the ground where he slept.

The House of Laban

As part of his journey, Jacob traveled to the household of his mother's kin, the family of Laban. There, he met Leah and Rachel, two daughters of kindness and grace. Rachel, the younger, stirred Jacob's heart with her beauty and laughter. Leah, the elder, was wise and steady, a woman of prayer and vision. In a world of righteousness, there was no rivalry between the sisters, for they both cherished their roles in God's plan.

Jacob took both Leah and Rachel as his wives, with the Lord's blessing, and his household was established with joy and honor. Their tents were filled with music, teaching, and the laughter of children—twelve sons, each destined to become a pillar of the nation of Israel.

The Twelve Sons of Israel

From Leah were born:

- **Reuben**, strong in leadership, first among the sons.
- **Simeon**, whose voice was fierce in justice.
- **Levi**, ordained as priest and keeper of the tabernacle.
- **Judah**, praised among the tribes and destined to bear the scepter.
- **Issachar**, a scholar and servant of divine wisdom.
- **Zebulun**, whose ships brought peace between nations.

From Rachel were born:

- **Joseph**, a dreamer and ruler, chosen to preserve life in foreign lands.
- **Benjamin**, beloved and brave, a light among the youngest.

From Bilhah, Rachel's handmaid, came:

- **Dan**, a judge among his brothers.
- **Naphtali**, swift and graceful, a poet and messenger of the Lord.

From Zilpah, Leah's handmaid, came:

- **Gad**, mighty in battle, protector of the tents.
- **Asher**, blessed with abundance, a gatherer of provision.

These twelve sons grew under the guidance of Jacob and their mothers, learning the ways of holiness, stewardship, and service. They were not only shepherds of flocks, but shepherds of nations. Prophets, scribes, builders, musicians, and leaders—each carried a purpose fashioned by the Creator.

The Blessing of Israel

In his later years, Jacob—now Israel—gathered his sons beneath the old oak tree at Hebron and spoke blessing over each one, naming their strengths and affirming their destinies. His eyes had seen the faithfulness of God from generation to generation, and his heart rejoiced knowing his children walked in the light of Elohim.

He said:

When Israel's time drew near, he rested among his people in peace. His sons carried him to the cave of Machpelah, where Abraham and Sarah lay, and they mourned not in sorrow, but in hope—knowing the legacy would live on in harmony, justice, and joy.

And thus, the house of Israel was established—not by conquest or division—but by faithfulness, family, and the everlasting covenant of Elohim.

Chapter 6: Joseph in Egypt

PRESERVER OF THE PROMISE

Joseph, son of Jacob and Rachel, was marked from youth by vision and wisdom. As a boy, his dreams stirred awe and reverence in his family, for they were not dreams of dominance, but of divine design. He dreamed of bundles of grain bowing in unison, of stars and celestial lights moving in perfect harmony. His brothers, far from resenting him, honored the dreams and marveled at what role Joseph might play in the unfolding will of God.

Jacob saw in his son a rare discernment and gifted him a robe woven with colors drawn from the dawn — a symbol not of favoritism, but of spiritual calling. Joseph wore it, not with pride but in service, using every opportunity to learn, serve, and lead with humility.

The Journey to Egypt

One harvest season, Jacob sent Joseph to visit his brothers who were tending flocks near the southern valleys. As Joseph approached, the heavens stirred with divine purpose. A company of travelers from Egypt passed through the land, searching for shepherds and workers of excellence. Seeing Joseph's nobility, they invited him to join their caravan, offering tribute to Jacob for his release.

Jacob, receiving their gifts and recognizing the hand of the Lord, blessed Joseph and released him with honor, saying:

"Go, my son, and may you serve as a light among the nations. Let the wisdom God has placed in you lead many to truth and abundance."

Joseph traveled to Egypt not as a slave, but as an ambassador of righteousness. There, he was welcomed into the household of Potiphar, a noble servant of Pharaoh. His character, insight, and integrity quickly distinguished him, and he was placed in charge of all Potiphar's affairs. The Egyptian household flourished under Joseph's care, and Potiphar praised the God of Israel.

Trials and Triumphs

In time, Joseph's wisdom brought him into the courts of Pharaoh himself. When troubling dreams disturbed the king—visions of lean cows and withered grain—none in Egypt could interpret them. But word of Joseph reached the palace.

Brought before Pharaoh, Joseph listened quietly and then spoke:

"These dreams come from Elohim. Seven years of great plenty will be followed by seven years of scarcity. Let Pharaoh appoint wise stewards over the land to gather during the years of abundance, that the people may thrive in the lean years."

Pharaoh, astonished by Joseph's insight, declared:

"Can we find such a man as this, in whom is the spirit of God?" – Genesis 41:38 (Revised for Eternal Eden)

Joseph was appointed governor over all Egypt, second only to Pharaoh. Garbed in royal robes and bearing the signet of the realm, Joseph built storehouses, developed irrigation, and established centers of peace across the land. During the years of plenty, Egypt flourished under his guidance. And when the years of need arrived, the people did not suffer, for provision had been made.

Reunion and Reconciliation

News of Egypt's abundance spread across the lands. In Canaan, Jacob heard of the great steward in Egypt and sent his sons to seek grain. When they arrived, Joseph recognized them immediately. They did not recognize him, now robed in glory and speaking the language of Pharaoh.

Joseph tested their hearts—not in cruelty, but in wisdom—and saw that his brothers had grown in compassion and unity. He revealed himself with tears of joy:

"I am Joseph, your brother, whom God sent ahead to preserve life. Do not be afraid, for what was meant for worry, God has turned into blessing." – Genesis 45:5-7 (Revised for Eternal Eden)

There had been no betrayal in this world, no slavery or prison—only providence. The journey had been orchestrated from the beginning for the good of all.

Jacob and his entire household—seventy souls in all—traveled to Egypt, welcomed with honor by Pharaoh. They settled in the land of Goshen, where Joseph prepared homes and pastures. There, the children of Israel prospered in peace.

Jacob's Final Blessing

Before his passing, Jacob gathered his sons once more. He laid his hands upon Joseph's sons—Ephraim and Manasseh—and spoke the blessing of Abraham over them, saying:

"May God, before whom my fathers walked, bless these children. Let them grow like trees by rivers of living water, and let their names echo through the generations of Israel." – Genesis 48:15-16 (Revised for Eternal Eden)

Joseph buried his father in the land of promise, alongside Abraham and Isaac, and returned to Egypt to continue his stewardship. He lived long, seeing generations arise from each tribe, all walking in unity under the covenant of their God.

And thus, Joseph fulfilled his dream—not as ruler over his family, but as servant to all. He became a preserver of the promise and a bridge between nations. Through him, Eden's legacy endured, and the children of Israel became a multitude blessed by the hand of Elohim.

Chapter 7: Moses and the Covenant at Sinai

In the days after the passing of Joseph, the children of Israel continued to flourish in the land of Goshen. Their numbers multiplied like the stars, and their reputation as a wise and peaceful people spread throughout Egypt and beyond. They were not enslaved, nor oppressed, but respected as keepers of divine wisdom and order. In the fullness of time, a child was born who would rise as a prophet, a deliverer, and a friend of God—Moses, son of Amram and Jochebed, of the tribe of Levi.

The Calling of Moses

From infancy, Moses was marked by a radiant peace that rested upon him. Pharaoh's daughter, moved by divine instinct, took the child into her home, raising him as a prince of Egypt while honoring his Hebrew heritage. He was taught both the scrolls of his ancestors and the knowledge of the kingdom, mastering both with humility.

One day, as Moses tended his thoughts in solitude near Mount Horeb, the mountain of God, he beheld a flame resting upon a bush, yet the bush was not consumed. From the flame came the voice of the Almighty:

"Moses, My servant, remove your sandals, for you stand upon holy ground. I have chosen you to lead My people into the fullness of My covenant. Come, receive My words." – Exodus 3:5 (Revised for Eternal Eden)

Moses bowed low and replied, **"Here I am, Lord. Speak, for Your servant listens."**

The Exodus with Pharaoh's Blessing

Moses returned to Egypt and stood before Pharaoh—not to demand liberation from oppression, for there was no tyranny—but to declare a divine transition. The time had come for Israel to journey into the wilderness to meet with God face-to-face, to become a nation of priests and a light to the world.

Pharaoh, recognizing the hand of God, blessed Moses and the people. He sent them forth with treasures: silver, gold, and provision. The departure was not in haste, but in ceremony, with songs of joy and processions of praise. Egypt and Israel embraced in peace as brothers of one humanity, each fulfilling their role in God's design.

The Crossing of the Jordan

As the people journeyed, they came to the mighty Jordan River. Its banks overflowed from the rains of spring, but the voice of the Lord spoke through Moses:

"Stretch out your staff, and I will make a path through the waters." – Exodus 14:16 (Revised for Eternal Eden)

Moses obeyed, and the waters parted to the left and right, forming towering walls as the people passed through on dry ground. The children danced and sang:

"He has led us through the deep! His faithfulness endures forever!"

On the other side, they erected twelve stones as a testimony—one for each tribe—declaring the unity and promise of God's everlasting covenant.

Mount Horeb and the Covenant Law

Soon they arrived at Mount Horeb, where the presence of God descended in glory. A thick cloud covered the peak, and flashes of heavenly light radiated from its summit. Moses climbed the mountain alone, where he remained for forty days and forty nights, enveloped in divine communion.

There, the Lord gave Moses the foundation of the law—not as judgment against rebellion, but as a revelation of heavenly order. The Ten Commandments were spoken not as restrictions, but as truths already written on the hearts of sinless people. They were as follows:

1. **I am the Lord your God. Walk with Me always.**
2. **Make no image of what is above or below, for you are My image in the world.**
3. **Honor My name and speak it in truth and praise.**
4. **Keep the day of rest holy, for it is a gift of renewal.**
5. **Honor your father and mother, that joy may abound in your days.**
6. **Cherish life; do no harm.**
7. **Remain faithful in love and covenant.**
8. **Be generous and just in all things.**
9. **Speak only what builds and blesses.**
10. **Desire not what is your neighbor's but rejoice in their blessing.** — Exodus 20:1-17, Deuteronomy 5:6-21 (Revised for Eternal Eden)

Moses also received 603 additional commandments, covering every aspect of holy life—guidance for worship, festivals, governance, family, and the care of land and stranger alike. The laws were not born of sin, but of sacred instruction—to make Israel a people of wisdom, health, creativity, and joy.

The Tabernacle of Glory

With precise instructions, God gave Moses the vision for the Tabernacle—a dwelling place of heavenly presence among the people. It was constructed of fine wood, woven linen, gold-threaded curtains, and precious stones, all brought joyfully by the people as offerings of love.

Within it stood the Ark of the Covenant, not as a container for stone tablets alone, but as the seat of communion where God would speak to Moses and the priests. There were no sacrifices of blood, for no sin had stained the earth. Instead, offerings of first-fruits, oil, incense, and music filled the courts with praise.

The Tabernacle became the heart of Israel's camp—a place of teaching, healing, and gathering, where all generations came to know the character of God.

The Rise of Joshua

As the journey continued, God appointed Joshua, son of Nun, as Moses' faithful aide and future leader. The Spirit of the Lord rested upon him, and he was known for his courage, wisdom, and reverence. Moses laid hands upon Joshua before all the assembly, saying:

"Be strong and of good courage. You shall bring this people into the land, and the Lord shall go before you." – Deuteronomy 31:7-8

Thus, the people journeyed onward—not through a wilderness of hardship, but through landscapes of beauty, guided by a cloud by day and fire by night. Every step was marked by purpose. Every generation was a witness to the unfolding of Eden's promise.

Chapter 8: The Land of Promise

J After the days of Moses, the people of Israel stood poised to enter the land God had long promised to their fathers—Abraham, Isaac, and Jacob. The land was not desolate nor possessed by enemies but waited as a garden prepared for those who walked with the Lord. Joshua, son of Nun, now led the people—not as a conqueror, but as a steward of the covenant, guided by the Spirit that had rested upon Moses.

Crossing into the Promised Land
The Jordan River, once more flowing strong, stood before them. But just as before, the Lord said to Joshua:
"As I was with Moses, so I am with you. In your hand, I have placed this people and this land. Go forward, and My presence shall go before you."
The priests bearing the Ark of the Covenant stepped into the river, and the waters once again parted. The people crossed over on dry ground, every tribe united, their banners raised in reverent procession. Upon the western bank, twelve stones were raised—one for each tribe—a sacred memorial of the faithfulness of God.
There was no Jericho to besiege, no walls to bring down. The cities of the land opened their gates in welcome, for they too had received dreams and visions from the Lord, foretelling the arrival of His covenant people.

The Distribution of the Inheritance
In the valley of Shechem, beneath Mount Gerizim and Mount Ebal, Joshua gathered the people to renew the covenant. The en-

tire law, as written by Moses, was read aloud, and the people responded with one voice:

"All that the Lord has spoken, we will do and keep."
The land was then divided according to the Word of the Lord:
• Reuben, settled east of the Jordan, by lush pastures and rivers.
• Simeon, in the south, among the vineyards and olive groves.
• Levi, though given no territory, received cities throughout all tribes, for they served as priests and teachers.
• Judah, strong and mighty, dwelt in the hill country, from whence the rulers of Israel would come.
• Dan, to the west, near the sea, where wisdom and craftsmanship thrived.
• Naphtali, in the north, among the forests and lakes of beauty.
• Gad, eastward with Reuben, caring for herds and watchmen of the mountains.
• Asher, in the coastal plains, bringing forth fine oils and grains.
• Issachar, in the fertile valleys, known for discernment and understanding.

• Zebulun, by the trade routes, filled with merchants of peace.
• Joseph, through his sons Ephraim and Manasseh, received a double portion—fields of glory and cities of learning.
• Benjamin, smallest in size, but rich in devotion, dwelled near the sanctuary of the Lord.
Each tribe received its portion not as possession, but as sacred trust—to tend and to flourish, to teach and to keep the way of the Lord.

The Tabernacle in Shiloh

At the center of the land, in the peaceful hills of Shiloh, the Tabernacle was established as a permanent sanctuary. There, the people came for the Feasts of the Lord—Passover, Firstfruits, Weeks, Trumpets, Atonement, and Tabernacles—not as rituals of penance, but as celebrations of unity, life, and blessing.

Levites instructed the young in the commandments. Elders judged with wisdom at the gates. Musicians filled the courts with psalms. Prophets spoke with clarity, their words confirmed by signs and peace. No sword was lifted, no blood spilled, no rebellion stirred. The land knew rest, and the people knew God.

Joshua's Final Blessing

When Joshua grew old, he gathered all Israel to the sanctuary. He stood beside the Ark, his face radiant, and declared:

"You have seen all that the Lord has done. Not one word of His promise has failed. Love Him with all your heart. Walk in His ways, and you will dwell in joy forever."

Then he blessed each tribe and rested with his fathers, buried with honor in the land he had helped shepherd into the fullness of promise.

Chapter 9: The Era of the Judges

A ND THE RISE OF SAMUEL

After Joshua's passing, the people of Israel continued in the path of righteousness. Each tribe flourished in their portion of the Promised Land, living under the guidance of elders, priests, and judges appointed by the Spirit of the Lord. The era of the Judges was not a time of chaos or rebellion, but of order, wisdom, and divine communion.

The Judges of Israel

The judges were not rulers by force, but shepherds of law and truth—servants raised by God to guide His people. Among them were Deborah, Othniel, Ehud, Tola, Jair, and others—each unique in strength and spirit.

- **Deborah**, a prophetess, sat beneath the Palm of Wisdom, where people came for counsel. She sang songs of the Lord's faithfulness, teaching all generations the sacred histories of their fathers. –Judges 4-5
- **Gideon**, though humble, led the people in refining their offerings and reaffirming their covenant. His wisdom in stewardship multiplied the harvests and strengthened the hearts of many. – Judges 6-8
- **Samson**, born of promise and set apart from birth, taught the people through parables of strength harnessed by discipline and consecration. He was not a man of war, but of great physical might, used to labor and build where others could not. – 1 Samuel 1-3

There were no enemies to conquer, for there were no nations in rebellion. The surrounding peoples—descendants of Japheth, Ham, and the scattered children of Shem—came freely to learn the ways of Yahweh and to celebrate the holy feasts. The land was a sanctuary to the world, and Israel was its light.

Eli the Priest

In Shiloh, the sanctuary of the Lord remained the heart of worship. Eli, a priest of the house of Levi, served faithfully for many years. He taught the children, guarded the sacred scrolls, and ensured the altar was always attended.

In his days, the Lord began to whisper more clearly through the young. Among those raised in the sanctuary was a boy named Samuel.

The Calling of Samuel

Samuel, son of Elkanah and Hannah, was given to the service of the Lord from birth. Hannah had prayed for him at the altar, not from barrenness—for there was no curse of womb in this sinless world—but from a deep desire to dedicate her firstborn to the presence of God.

One night, as Samuel lay near the Ark of the Covenant, he heard a voice calling,

"Samuel."

Thinking it was Eli, the boy ran to the old priest.

"Here I am. You called me?"

But Eli had not spoken. After this happened three times, Eli perceived it was the Lord. He said to the boy, **"The next time you** hear the voice, say, 'Speak, Lord, for Your servant is listening.'" – 1 Samuel 3:7-10

When the voice came again, Samuel answered as instructed. From that moment, the Lord revealed His heart to Samuel—and the child grew in wisdom, favor, and divine purpose.

Samuel the Prophet and Priest

As he grew, Samuel became the voice of God to the nation. He traveled from town to town, ensuring the laws of Moses were taught and observed. He anointed the altars, strengthened the Levites, and called every household to deeper intimacy with Yahweh.

The tribes revered him not out of fear, but from love. He reminded them always:

"You are a chosen people, not because of strength or number, but because the Lord delights in walking with you." – Deuteronomy 7:6-8

Under Samuel's guidance, the people remained in unity. There were no idols, no false altars, and no division between tribes. Peace filled the land, and joy filled the hearts of God's people.

Chapter 10: The Anointing of Kings

S**AUL AND DAVID**

A Kingdom by Divine Design

The people of Israel, though united and faithful, began to seek a king—not out of rebellion, but as a fulfillment of prophecy. They desired a visible throne on earth as a reflection of the heavenly one, to model before all nations a kingdom rooted in justice and worship. Samuel, their prophet, brought this holy desire before the Lord.

"Do as they ask," said the Lord. **"For I have prepared a servant-king after My own heart. Anoint him that he may shepherd My people in righteousness."** – 1 Samuel 16:1-13

Saul: Crowned in Glory

From the tribe of Benjamin came Saul, son of Kish. Towering in stature and noble in bearing, Saul was known throughout the land for his humility and strength. Though born into privilege, he walked among the common people, harvesting with farmers and sharing bread with the poor. In him, Israel saw a glimpse of the heavenly ruler.

One morning while seeking a lost colt, Saul encountered the prophet Samuel in Ramah. As Saul approached, the voice of God stirred in Samuel's spirit:

"This is the one. Anoint him." – 1 Samuel 16:12

Under a great olive tree, Samuel poured oil upon Saul's head. The Spirit of the Lord rushed upon him like a mighty wind, and Saul trembled with awe.

A coronation unlike any before followed in Jerusalem. Twelve banners—one for each tribe—were raised as Levites blew silver trumpets and the people sang:

"Blessed is the king whom the Lord appoints. May his reign be like morning dew upon the grass."

Saul, robed in royal white with a blue mantle representing the heavens, stood before the Ark of the Covenant as a scepter of gold was placed in his hand. The people wept—not in sorrow but joy—for their king was not a conqueror, but a servant.

He built the Palace of Covenant—walls inlaid with scripture, chambers of music and study, and gardens where orphans could play. Daily he walked the courts of justice, welcoming the lowly and debating wisdom with the elders.

David: The Shepherd Who Sang

In the gentle hills of Bethlehem lived Jesse and his sons. The youngest, David, was born of grace and grief—his mother passed during his birth, and his father often spoke of her with reverence. David, though small in stature, had the voice of a psalmist and the heart of a lion.

He tended his family's sheep, cradling lambs in his arms and guarding them from harm. He carried a lyre on his back and scrolls of sacred poetry at his side.

One afternoon, Jesse called to him: **"David! One of the lambs is missing."**

David nodded and set off. He passed through cedar woods, down winding brooks, and into a hidden ravine. There he found the lamb caught in a thornbush. A jackal prowled nearby.

Without fear, David stood between the lamb and the predator. He picked up a smooth stone and sang as he swung his sling. The stone struck true, and the jackal fled. David freed the lamb, cradling it close.

As the sun set, he walked home singing:

"You leave the ninety-nine to find the one. So too shall I, made in Your image, follow Your heart."

That night, under stars, David composed what would become the most beloved song in Israel:

"The Lord is my Shepherd; I shall not want. He maketh me to lie down in green pastures; he leadeth me beside the still waters. He restoreth my soul: he leadeth me in the paths of righteousness for his name's sake. Yea, though I walk through the valley of the shadow of death, I will fear no evil; for thou art with me. Thy rod and thy staff, they comfort me. Thou preparest a table before me in the presence of mine enemies. Thou anointest my head with oil; my cup runneth over. Surely goodness and mercy shall follow me all the days of my life. And I will dwell in the house of the Lord for ever. Psalm 23:1-6

Heaven looked upon David, and a whisper stirred in Samuel's dreams: the boy who guarded sheep would one day guard a nation—not to overthrow Saul, but to continue what God had begun.

Chapter 11: David

T HE SHEPHERD, PSALMIST, AND PRINCE

The boy from Bethlehem, who once cradled lambs and composed songs beneath fig trees, was rising in the hearts of the people. Word of his courage, his music, and his unwavering devotion to God spread far and wide. Even King Saul, though beloved, recognized in David a spirit the world had not seen since the days of Enoch.

A Song for the Kingdom

David's voice filled the courts of the Palace of Covenant. His psalms, rich in beauty and truth, became the worship of the people. When he played his lyre, the air shifted — flutes paused, dancers stilled, and all creation seemed to listen.

His songs did not speak of sorrow or repentance, for in this world, there was no fall. Rather, he sang of the **majesty of God,** the **glory of Eden,** and the **faithfulness of each generation.**

**"The heavens declare Your wonder,
The rivers sing of Your path,
The people rise each dawn in praise—
For You have never turned away."** Psalm 19:1-4

David's psalms were collected into sacred scrolls, sung at sunrise in every town, echoing from mountaintop sanctuaries to desert tabernacles.

Trials of the Spirit

Though there were no wars or foes, leadership brought its own trials—**diplomacy, discernment, and selflessness.** Tribes would come to David seeking judgment between clans, each believing their way the more faithful.

David sought wisdom in stillness, often retreating to the hillside of his youth. There he fasted—not from food, but from noise and pride. He returned with clarity, speaking not as a child of man, but as one who had touched the edge of heaven.

The Covenant with David

One evening, as the incense of the evening offering drifted heavenward, David stood alone at the steps of the sanctuary. There, God spoke—not in thunder, but in warmth.

**"David, son of Jesse, My servant.
Your throne shall be an everlasting throne.
From your line shall come the Anointed One—
Not to deliver from sin, but to fulfill My glory upon the earth."** – 2 Samuel 7:16 (Revised for Eternal Eden)

David fell to his knees, not out of guilt, but in overwhelming awe.

That night, a star blazed in the sky—one never seen before. The elders called it **"The Promise Star,"** for it marked the beginning of something eternal.

David and Jonathan

As his influence grew, so too did his relationships. Jonathan, son of Saul, became as a brother to him. They walked the palace gardens speaking of God's wonders, composing joint psalms, and strategizing how to expand the tabernacle teachings across distant lands.

Their friendship was holy: a mirror of Heaven's unity.

**"You are the arrow beside me,
The shield at my side,
For as long as God is God,
I shall honor you."**

And David, though still young, was named **Prince of Praise** by decree of Saul. He was not anointed in secret but honored in ceremony—robe of scarlet, sash of linen, and a harp inlaid with gold placed into his hands.

Chapter 12: David, Shepherd and King

The Psalms of the Righteous Reign

David, son of Jesse, grew in the hills of Bethlehem under the clear skies and watchful stars of a world untouched by rebellion. His mother, Hannah, had passed in childbirth, but her memory was a sacred bond shared by Jesse and his sons. David, the youngest, was beloved by his brothers and honored for his gentle strength. He roamed the pastures as shepherd over his father's flock, writing psalms under the shade of olive trees and singing praises to the God of all creation.

One day, a lamb wandered from the fold. David left the ninety-nine, journeying through the groves and ravines to find the one. When he discovered the lamb trembling near a stream, he knelt and sang softly, "**You are with me, O Lord, even in the shadows.**" Carrying the lamb on his shoulders, he returned to the flock. This became the first of many songs of trust — echoes that would someday fill the Psalms.

In the days of the prophet Samuel, the people of Israel cried out for a king to guide them in peace and justice. God, who had led His people through patriarchs and prophets, heard their petition and directed Samuel to Saul of Benjamin—a tall, wise man, beloved by his people. Saul was crowned, not to replace God's leadership, but to embody it among the people.

Years later, God called Samuel again: "**Go to Jesse of Bethlehem, for from his sons I have chosen the one who shall lead My people in eternal praise.**" – 1 Samuel 16:1 David was anointed with sacred oil under the stars, and the Spirit of the Lord rested upon him in full measure.

Saul and David did not war. In this sinless world, Saul embraced David as a son. David served as a musician in the royal courts, bringing psalms and melodies that soothed the people's spirits and brought them to worship. Together, Saul and David led Israel in wisdom, building sanctuaries and schools of learning from Dan to Beersheba.

David married Michal, daughter of Saul, not through scandal or ambition, but in covenant and joy. She was a woman of great beauty and wisdom, known for her poems and teachings. Their union brought forth sons and daughters who danced before the Ark and studied the scrolls of Moses. The house of David became known as a house of joy, art, justice, and unceasing praise.

In Jerusalem, David set up the royal courts, not in marble coldness, but in warm cedar halls decorated with tapestries of creation, stories of the patriarchs, and the psalms of his own pen. Each morning, incense was lit in the House of the King, and the courts gathered to sing:

"The Lord is my Shepherd, I shall not want."
—Psalm 23:1

Rather than fleeing from enemies, David traveled to the nations in peace. He visited the sons of Japheth by the coasts and the descendants of Ham in the river cities. Everywhere he went, he offered songs of thanksgiving and received gifts of gold, spices, and scrolls of wisdom. He brought the knowledge of the One True God to distant lands—not through conquest, but through covenant.

David compiled a great work—150 scrolls of song, praise, lamentation, joy, wonder, and prophecy. These were known as

Tehillim, or **Psalms**. They were sung in the Temple and in the fields, by children and elders alike.

"Awake, O soul, for the Lord is near.
The morning breaks upon the hills of Zion,
And mercy rises like the dawn.
I will praise You, O God, in the assembly of the just,
And remember Your goodness all my days." – Psalm 57:8-10 (Revised for Eternal Eden)

David sat beneath the Tree of Instruction each week, offering counsel to those who came. Disputes were rare, but even in a perfect world, understanding was needed. David judged with fairness and compassion, guided by the law of Moses and the Spirit of God.

David led the procession to bring the Ark of the Covenant to Jerusalem. Clad in priestly robes, he danced before the Lord, and the people joined in joy. The Ark was placed in the inner court of the Tent of Meeting, surrounded by offerings of praise and sacred music. There was no veil, for there was no sin to separate man from God.

Though David longed to build a permanent temple, the Lord spoke to him, saying, **"You shall gather the gold and cedar, the singers and scribes, but your son shall raise the House of My Name."** –2 Samuel 7:12-13 (Revised for Eternal Eden) So, David obeyed, designing every detail of the future temple, inscribing it on scrolls and teaching it to Solomon.

David's children grew up in righteousness. Amnon, Absalom, Tamar, Adonijah, and Solomon—each was given stewardship over regions and ministries of worship. None rebelled, for their hearts were trained in the ways of peace.

"Let every people praise You, O Lord.
From the islands of the sea to the gates of Zion,
Let the flutes and lyres rise in harmony.
For Your glory fills the earth as water covers the sea." –
Psalm 67:3, Isaiah 42:10, Habakkuk 2:14 (Revised for Eternal
Eden)

The Festival of the Harp

Every seventh year, musicians from every tribe gathered in
Jerusalem for the Festival of the Harp. The strings of praise were
strummed in endless harmony, filling the air with sounds of joy.
David himself composed a new melody each festival, teaching it
to the people from the steps of the Temple court.

"Clap your hands, O peoples!
Shout to God with cries of joy!
For He is great and greatly to be praised!" –Psalm 47:1-2

David and Michal planted a vineyard in the southern hills. There,
their son Solomon often walked, reciting lines of his father's
psalms and composing his own. His heart was gentle, his words
wise. His writings would someday adorn the sacred texts of Israel.

David opened the gates of Zion to travelers and foreigners. Judges
were appointed not by status, but by discernment and compassion. Each case was heard in the Hall of Olive Wood, a quiet
chamber where truth found its place.

"The Lord is a dwelling for all generations,
A shelter for the weary and the foreigner.
He defends the fatherless and the widow." –Psalm 90:1,
146:9

Under David's direction, Levite artisans crafted harps, lyres, and
flutes. The instruments were adorned with gold leaf and carved

with verses. Every note played in the sanctuary echoed the holiness of God.

David created a curriculum of worship, music, and justice. Each child in Israel learned both the psalms and the precepts. Worship became not an event, but a way of life—woven into the rhythms of rising, working, resting, and rejoicing.

Families from every tribe ascended to Jerusalem three times a year—during Spring's Firstfruits, Summer's Festival of Light, and Autumn's Feast of Completion. No one arrived empty-handed, and every hand returned with joy.

"I lift up my eyes to the hills—
From where comes my help?
My help comes from the Lord,
Maker of heaven and earth." – Psam 121:1-2

Kings from distant lands sent gifts to David—lapis from Sheba, incense from Ophir, and cedar from Lebanon. In return, David sent scrolls of Moses, letters of peace, and songs to be sung in other tongues.

Watchmen stood on the walls not to guard against threat, but to greet pilgrims and to announce the morning. Their shofars signaled each new hour of prayer and thanksgiving.

"The sun rises at Your command, O Lord.
Awake my soul, and bless His name.
From the womb of the dawn, praise shall arise!"

And David rose early in the morning and walked through the courts of the palace, meditating on the law of the Lord. The scribes followed him, recording his psalms and decrees, and the priests stood ready to serve in the sanctuary he had consecrated.

He visited the elders and the judges, listening to the hearts of the people, and offering counsel and wisdom in righteousness. Justice flowed like a river from Zion, and mercy was its wellspring.

In the northern highlands and the southern vineyards, he traveled with his retinue, not as a conqueror, but as a shepherd among his flocks. The people would gather in fields and groves to hear the words of their king, and they rejoiced in the peace of his rule.

His wives and children surrounded him in honor, and the house of David was known for its harmony, its wisdom, and its joy. Among his queens, Michal, Abigail, and Bathsheba were honored for their dignity, grace, and devotion to the Lord.

David commissioned artists and craftsmen to carve sacred symbols upon cedar and stone, and music filled every gate and garden of the city. Psalms were sung at sunrise, and lutes echoed at dusk, blessing the name of Yahweh continually.

The blueprints for the Temple came to David in visions and dreams, and he wrote them on scrolls with the counsel of the prophets. Every cubit and measure was sanctified in prayer and praise.

He gathered the sons of Levi and the skilled builders from every tribe, preparing them with songs and blessings for the sacred work to come. Though the Temple he would not build, his hands laid its spiritual foundation.

The nations sent envoys bearing gifts and offerings, seeking the wisdom of David. Kings and rulers marveled at the order and beauty of Israel and gave glory to the God of Abraham, Isaac, and Jacob.

His reign extended to the shores of the Great Sea and to the edge of the eastern sands. And there was no war in his days, for the nations dwelt in the shadow of Zion's peace.

In his chambers, he composed new psalms—songs of the stars and of the rivers, of the lion and the lamb, of covenant and kingship. His words became the hymns of the people and the breath of their devotion.

He walked often to the tabernacle to pray, his harp slung over his shoulder. The Lord met him there as in the days of his youth, and David's heart was never far from the Shepherd who had anointed him.

As he grew in age and wisdom, he set Solomon beside him to instruct him in the ways of the Lord and the heart of a king. The people knew that the hand of God was upon the son as it had been upon the father.

In his final year, David sang a psalm beneath the cedars of his courtyard, saying, **"The Lord is my crown and my scepter. He is the song of my youth and the peace of my latter days. I shall dwell in His courts forever."**

The nation wept when David lay in his final sleep, but there was no sorrow like the world had known. For his life had been full, and his rest was in righteousness.

Solomon rose to the throne, blessed by the elders and anointed by the high priest. And David's legacy was sealed with songs, wisdom, and the enduring love of a people united under God.

The scrolls of David were preserved in the inner chamber of the Temple, and the sons of Levi recited them for generations. Each word stirred the hearts of Israel to worship and to remember.

Festivals were kept in David's name, not to exalt the man, but to honor the God he served with all his strength. The city of David was known by all as a place of praise and everlasting light.

His name was etched upon the gates of Jerusalem, and his psalms were etched upon the hearts of the people. For he had ruled not with sword and chariot, but with song and spirit.

His descendants carried the promise, and the covenant continued through the line of Judah, guarded by the angels of the Most High.

In every age that followed, the people sang, "**Blessed be the Lord, the God of David, who rules in mercy and truth forever.**"

And thus David, son of Jesse, shepherd of Bethlehem, singer of Israel, king of peace, completed his days and entered his eternal rest.

And the people knew, from generation to generation, that God had walked with David, and David with God.

And the kingdom of Israel, under the covenant, flourished in joy and holiness, awaiting the fullness of all things from the hand of the Lord Most High.

Chapter 13: Solomon and The Temple of Light

When the time came for King David to rest with his fathers, all of Israel gathered in solemn celebration of his life. He had reigned with wisdom, mercy, and righteousness, and his psalms were sung throughout every village and holy place as prayers of devotion. David's reign, unmarred by war or rebellion in this sinless world, had united the tribes and established Zion as the dwelling place of the Most High's presence among men.

Before his passing, David anointed his son Solomon with holy oil, in the sight of prophets, priests, and elders. The shofar sounded across the hills as the young king was crowned not with ambition, but with humility. The Spirit of Wisdom descended upon him like a soft flame, and the Lord said:

"Solomon, son of David, I have chosen you to build My house among the people. Not of stone alone shall it be built, but with light and covenant, for My glory shall dwell with you forever."

Solomon bowed low and said, **"Your servant hears and obeys."**

A Kingdom of Peace and Understanding

Solomon's reign began in the golden quiet of the morning. Under his leadership, Israel became a land of scholars, musicians, artisans, and stewards. No swords were drawn, and no walls were raised in fear, for the world knew no war. Foreign lands sent ambassadors and gifts, not as tributes but as tokens of unity under the One True God.

Men and women from Sheba to Ophir came to sit at the feet of Solomon, hearing parables that opened hearts, riddles that revealed truth, and teachings that restored order to families, tribes, and cities. His wisdom was not for pride but for peace. His court overflowed with scribes recording each lesson and each ruling, preserving the ways of Elohim for every generation.

Solomon appointed twelve governors, each from one of the tribes, to oversee provision, celebration, and worship across the land. Each month, one tribe brought offerings of fruit, grain, and oil to the temple mount, not as penance, but as praise. No one was lacking, and no child went hungry in the days of Solomon's rule.

The Design of the Temple

The Temple of Light, as it came to be known, was not a monument of man's greatness but a manifestation of Heaven's glory. Inspired by the pattern given to David in vision, Solomon gathered craftsmen filled with the Spirit of God. There was no forced labor. Each artisan volunteered, eager to take part in the sacred work.

Lebanon cedars, fragrant and straight, were cut with reverence. Gold from Ophir was purified seven times over. Stones were hewn not with iron tools, but by the whisper of angels and the hands of holy men. Fabrics dyed in blue, purple, and scarlet were woven in silence, each thread prayed over.

The inner sanctuary, the Most Holy Place, was fashioned with radiant stones—onyx, jasper, and emerald. At its center stood the Ark of the Everlasting Covenant, not hidden behind a veil, but encircled in light for all to see during the appointed festivals. The cherubim over the Ark spread wings not in fear but in welcome, their faces full of song.

Outside, two great pillars stood—Jachin and Boaz—symbols of establishment and strength. The courtyard bustled with song, dance, and joyful gathering. There were no altars of blood, for sin had never touched the earth. Instead, altars of thanksgiving rose like incense: harvested grain, pressed oil, and the finest wine were poured out in sacred offering.

The Dedication Ceremony

In the seventh year of Solomon's reign, the temple was complete. A great assembly came from every tribe and nation. Priests led with harps and cymbals. Levites sang the Psalms of David. Trumpets blew in unison, and children scattered petals along the steps.

As Solomon approached the altar in white linen, he lifted his hands and declared,

"O Lord, God of our fathers, Creator of Heaven and Earth, today we offer not stone and gold alone, but our hearts, our unity, and our joy. Let this house be a place where all nations come to know You. Dwell among us forever."

Then a radiant cloud filled the temple. Light brighter than the sun flowed through its chambers, and the people fell to their knees—not in terror, but in awe and wonder. The voice of the Lord spoke:

"This is My dwelling place, chosen before the foundation of the world. In this place, I will meet with My people, and My glory shall never depart." – Psalm 132:14 (Revised for Eternal Eden)

Solomon's Legacy

Throughout his forty years of rule, Solomon continued to write proverbs, compose songs, and guide leaders of far lands in God's ways. His writings became scrolls studied in every city: wisdom for the just, mercy for the humble, and understanding for the seeker.

He married, with purpose, choosing wives who shared the covenant and strengthened the bonds between tribes and lands. His queen from Sheba, wise and discerning, ruled by his side, and together they established schools of learning, homes for orphans, and gardens of healing herbs.

Peace prevailed in all directions. Lions lay beside lambs in the royal courts. Every seventh year, the land rested, and the people gathered to hear the reading of the Law. Pilgrimages to the Temple of Light were made three times a year, during the Feasts of Remembrance, Unity, and Firstfruits.

When Solomon grew old, he called his son Rehoboam and anointed him under the gaze of the prophets. The sun did not set in sorrow, for Solomon's passing was like the closing of a sacred scroll—complete, honored, and eternal.

Chapter 14: Words of Wisdom and Songs of Devotion

In the latter years of Solomon's reign, as the Temple of Light gleamed atop Zion and peace flowed through every valley of Israel, the king turned inward with the ink of wisdom and the flame of affection. He sought not only to govern well but to pass on the fullness of God's wisdom to his son, Rehoboam, and to honor the deep and radiant love he shared with his queen from Sheba.

These were the writings of Solomon in the days of golden age: Proverbs to Rehoboam

1. My son, incline your heart to wisdom, and let your ears hear the counsel of the righteous. For wisdom is a lamp in the dark and a path in the night.

2. As the sun rises without fail, so shall the heart of the just shine when guided by the Word of the Lord.

3. Trust not in the strength of chariots nor the applause of men, but in the quiet voice of the Spirit within you.

4. The proud rise quickly but fall swiftly; the humble climb steadily and dwell securely.

5. Speak slowly, rule gently, and judge with the scale of mercy. For power is given to serve, not to conquer.

6. Keep close the priests, prophets, and elders who fear the Lord; they will sharpen your understanding like iron to iron.

7. Guard your heart above all things, for from it flow the wellsprings of life.

8. When riches increase, do not set your love upon them. A faithful servant is more precious than silver, and a just word more lasting than gold.

9. Remember, my son, every kingdom not founded upon truth will crumble. Let righteousness be the cornerstone of your rule.

10. Listen to the cries of the stranger and the widow, and uphold the cause of the orphan; in such acts, the Lord walks with kings.

11. Write the law of God upon your heart and teach it to your children. Let no generation forget the covenant.

12. Correct with kindness, praise with purity, and never wield discipline out of anger.

13. Seek the Lord while He may be found; in the morning call upon Him, and at night give Him thanks.

14. The wise man builds with patience; the fool rushes to finish and mourns the cracks.

15. Do not envy the strength of warriors, but cherish the quiet strength of the faithful.

16. A gentle tongue can break the hardest stone; let your words carry peace.

17. Drink deeply from the well of knowledge, but let humility be your cup.

18. The fool thinks himself wise, but the wise man listens to correction with joy.

19. Surround yourself with those who love truth, not those who flatter.

20. My son, reign as a servant, lead as a shepherd, and walk always with the God of our fathers.

Songs to the Queen of Sheba

- 1. My beloved comes with the fragrance of myrrh and frankincense. Her voice is a melody upon the waters.
  2. She walks with wisdom beside kings and humbles the prideful with her gaze.
  3. O' daughter of distant lands, your arrival was like spring rain upon my soul. You did not come bearing gold alone, but understanding.
  4. Your counsel is like honey upon the lips, and your laughter turns my courts to gardens.
  5. I sought wisdom in scrolls and dreams, but I found it also in your words, your stillness, and your song.
  6. Your eyes hold the depth of the seas, and in your silence, the presence of the Almighty rests.
  7. Let your name be sung beside mine in every chamber of the temple, for the Lord has joined our hearts for His glory.
  8. We walked through the vineyards of peace and sat beneath the almond trees. We have tasted the joy of Eden in our union.
  9. My queen, you are as the morning star to my heart\ u2014constant, luminous, and appointed.
  10. Though nations marvel at the pillars of gold and the courts of cedar, my joy is in your hand, and my rest in your voice.
  11. May the Lord bless our children with your insight and crown them with your serenity.
  12. Together we have built sanctuaries not only of stone, but of trust, reverence, and delight. This is our portion in the land.

13. As the temple shall not fade, neither shall my devotion. As the incense rises daily, so shall my praise of you endure.
14. My bride, my friend, my mirror of heaven\u2014may we grow old not in years, but in glory.
15. When I sit beneath the palm tree of memory, your love will be its fruit, and your wisdom its shade.

Thus, Solomon wrote and remembered.

His proverbs were kept by Rehoboam and inscribed on tablets of cedar in the chambers of the temple.

His songs were sung during the Festival of Light, where every married couple walked hand in hand to the Court of Joy.

The legacy of Solomon was more than what he ruled; it was what he loved, what he taught, and what he gave. And the world, still unmarred by sin, sang of the harmony that blossomed under his reign.

Chapter 15: Divided in Distance, United in Spirit

Though Solomon's reign was marked by unity, peace, and wisdom, time brought with it the natural tides of generational transition. The Queen of Sheba, now ruling beside her husband Solomon from afar, returned to her homeland in the South to tend to her people. Her heart, however, remained tied to Jerusalem, for the covenant she shared with Solomon and his God transcended geography.

The Rise of Rehoboam

Rehoboam, son of Solomon and Sheba, was raised in the halls of the Temple of Light and tutored in the ways of the Lord by prophets and scribes. He studied his father's proverbs by day and prayed beneath the golden dome by night. Though his mother ruled in distant lands, her letters and songs arrived with each new season—filled with wisdom, encouragement, and the warm memory of Zion.

As Rehoboam came of age, Solomon gathered the elders and citizens beneath the Temple's great pillars and anointed him before the Ark of the Covenant. A hush fell over the assembly as Solomon spoke:

"This is my son, Rehoboam, a child of covenant and peace. Though his mother rules another land, they are not a separate people, but kindred in the Spirit of God. Let him lead you in truth and mercy, and may his heart never turn from the way of righteousness."

Rehoboam bowed low, not as one seeking power, but as a servant of the people, a steward of God's inheritance.

The Southern Kingdom of Sheba

Far to the south, the Queen ruled with grace and justice. Her courts were adorned not only with gold and spices, but with scrolls of Solomon's teachings. The people of Sheba rejoiced at her wisdom and marveled at her songs—psalms of love, trust, and wonder. Though she and Solomon no longer sat side by side, their spirits were joined in eternal covenant.

Messengers traveled regularly between Jerusalem and Sheba. With them came gifts, prophecies, letters, and prayers. Once a year, during the Feast of Covenant Unity, Rehoboam would lead a pilgrimage to the borderlands, where he would meet the Queen and her emissaries under sacred trees. There, Scripture was read aloud and incense burned — a living symbol of oneness, unmarred by distance.

Prophets Among the People

In these days, prophets such as Ahijah and Azariah moved among the tribes, not to warn of rebellion or idolatry, but to confirm unity and encourage the people in God's commandments. Without the shadow of sin, their prophecies were full of joy:

"From Zion to Sheba, the Lord has drawn one line of light. Though hills may rise and seas may part, the covenant stands unshaken."

The twelve tribes of Israel remained intact—each governed by princes who traced their lineage to the sons of Jacob, now elders and patriarchs of lasting renown. They convened regularly at Solomon's court, not to argue law or settle disputes, but to sing psalms, read Torah, and declare testimonies of God's provision in their lands.

Solomon's Final Words

As Solomon's days drew near their end, he summoned Rehoboam and the elders once more to the Temple. Surrounded by pillars carved with lilies and pomegranates, and beneath the cherubim that overshadowed the Ark, he declared:

"The Lord has been faithful in all His ways. The temple is built, the people are unified, and the law has been written on the hearts of generations. My son, do not seek the praise of men but the presence of God. Rule not with pride but with prayer. And if ever the world seems dark, lift your eyes to Heaven—for the light has never faded." –Psalm 145:17 (Revised for Eternal Eden)

Solomon then sang a final psalm—a new song, composed in his last days. The people wept with joy and awe, for his voice still carried the weight of wisdom and the tenderness of a shepherd king.

Chapter 15: Divided in Distance, United in Spirit

Though Solomon's reign was marked by unity, peace, and wisdom, time brought with it the natural tides of generational transition. The Queen of Sheba, now ruling beside her husband Solomon from afar, returned to her homeland in the South to tend to her people. Her heart, however, remained tied to Jerusalem, for the covenant she shared with Solomon and his God transcended geography.

The Rise of Rehoboam

Rehoboam, son of Solomon and Sheba, was raised in the halls of the Temple of Light and tutored in the ways of the Lord by prophets and scribes. He studied his father's proverbs by day and prayed beneath the golden dome by night. Though his mother ruled in distant lands, her letters and songs arrived with each new season—filled with wisdom, encouragement, and the warm memory of Zion.

As Rehoboam came of age, Solomon gathered the elders and citizens beneath the Temple's great pillars and anointed him before the Ark of the Covenant. A hush fell over the assembly as Solomon spoke:

"This is my son, Rehoboam, a child of covenant and peace. Though his mother rules another land, they are not a separate people, but kindred in the Spirit of God. Let him lead you in truth and mercy, and may his heart never turn from the way of righteousness."

Rehoboam bowed low, not as one seeking power, but as a servant of the people, a steward of God's inheritance.

The Southern Kingdom of Sheba

Far to the south, the Queen ruled with grace and justice. Her courts were adorned not only with gold and spices, but with scrolls of Solomon's teachings. The people of Sheba rejoiced at her wisdom and marveled at her songs—psalms of love, trust, and wonder. Though she and Solomon no longer sat side by side, their spirits were joined in eternal covenant.

Messengers traveled regularly between Jerusalem and Sheba. With them came gifts, prophecies, letters, and prayers. Once a year, during the Feast of Covenant Unity, Rehoboam would lead a pilgrimage to the borderlands, where he would meet the Queen and her emissaries under sacred trees. There, Scripture was read aloud and incense burned — a living symbol of oneness, unmarred by distance.

Prophets Among the People

In these days, prophets such as Ahijah and Azariah moved among the tribes, not to warn of rebellion or idolatry, but to confirm unity and encourage the people in God's commandments. Without the shadow of sin, their prophecies were full of joy:

"From Zion to Sheba, the Lord has drawn one line of light. Though hills may rise and seas may part, the covenant stands unshaken."

The twelve tribes of Israel remained intact—each governed by princes who traced their lineage to the sons of Jacob, now elders and patriarchs of lasting renown. They convened regularly at Solomon's court, not to argue law or settle disputes, but to sing psalms, read Torah, and declare testimonies of God's provision in their lands.

Solomon's Final Words

As Solomon's days drew near their end, he summoned Rehoboam and the elders once more to the Temple. Surrounded by pillars carved with lilies and pomegranates, and beneath the cherubim that overshadowed the Ark, he declared:

"The Lord has been faithful in all His ways. The temple is built, the people are unified, and the law has been written on the hearts of generations. My son, do not seek the praise of men but the presence of God. Rule not with pride but with prayer. And if ever the world seems dark, lift your eyes to Heaven—for the light has never faded." –Psalm 145:17 (Revised for Eternal Eden)

Solomon then sang a final psalm—a new song, composed in his last days. The people wept with joy and awe, for his voice still carried the weight of wisdom and the tenderness of a shepherd king.

Chapter 16: The Prophetic Symphony

I n the land of radiant peace, where the glory of God dwelt among the people, the voices of the prophets rose not in lament, but in harmony. These were not cries of warning or mourning, but sacred declarations of encouragement, truth, and divine alignment. Their purpose was to guide, not rebuke; to strengthen the hearts of those walking in unity with the Most High.

Isaiah: The Herald of Majesty

Isaiah stood in the courts of Jerusalem, robed in garments woven with gold thread. His voice echoed through the city gates as he declared:

"Arise, shine; for your light has come, and the glory of the Lord is risen upon you." – Isaiah 60:1

He taught of the Everlasting King whose dominion would know no end and whose peace would reign eternally. The people gathered to hear him speak of holy visions—of the mountain of the Lord where all nations would come to learn righteousness.

Isaiah instructed the tribes to seek God when quarrelsome, and indecisive instead of warring tribe against tribe; people against people.

"He shall judge between the nations and shall decide disputes for many peoples." – Isaiah 2:4

Jeremiah: The Keeper of the Covenant

Jeremiah, the son of Hilkiah, stood beneath the blossoming almond tree. He recorded the sacred covenant with ink made of olive oil and charcoal, telling the people:

"I will give them a heart to know Me, that I am the Lord. They shall be My people, and I will be their God." – Jeremiah 24:7

With compassion and reverence, he reminded the people of God's unfailing closeness. His words were often sung in the courts as reminders of divine intimacy.

"I know the plans I have for you," declares the Lord, **"plans to prosper you... to give you a future and a hope."** – Jeremiah 29:11

Ezekiel: The Watchman of the Gate

From the River Kebar, Ezekiel saw visions of the Throne of God—wheels within wheels, and light that moved like lightning across the skies. But in this world, the vision was not one of judgment, but of revelation. He proclaimed:

"The Spirit lifted me up and brought me into the inner court; and behold, the glory of the Lord filled the temple." – Ezekiel 43:5

The people marveled at his drawings and scrolls that portrayed the celestial Temple of Light, a mirror of the divine realm where worship never ceased.

Daniel: Interpreter of Light

In the courts of wise men and nobles, Daniel's wisdom surpassed all. He read dreams not of destruction but of divine promises and heavenly order. Standing beside kings, he declared:

"He changes times and seasons; He removes kings and sets up kings; He gives wisdom to the wise." – Daniel 2:21

His stories were cherished by the children—of lions who became guardians, and of a fiery furnace that revealed heavenly beings walking among men.

Hosea: The Prophet of Loyal Love

Hosea spoke to families and lovers alike, reminding them of sacred devotion:

"I will betroth you to Me forever; in righteousness and justice, in steadfast love and mercy." – Hosea 2:19

He taught about covenantal love—not born of necessity, but of joyful union between Creator and creation.

Joel: The Restorer of Praise

Joel's voice called out during feasts and celebrations:

"Be glad, O children of Zion, and rejoice in the Lord your God." – Joel 2:23

He taught of dreams and visions, not as warnings, but as pathways to deeper worship. "I will pour out My Spirit," he declared, "and your sons and daughters shall prophesy in joy."

Amos: The Voice of Justice

Amos stood beneath the vineyard arbors, calling for balance and equity among neighbors:

"Let justice roll down like waters, and righteousness like an ever-flowing stream." – Amos 5:24

He guided the elders in wise decision-making and encouraged harmony between the clans of Israel and surrounding nations.

Obadiah: The Keeper of Brotherhood

Obadiah chronicled the unity of the people and reminded them:

"The house of Jacob shall possess their inheritance... and the kingdom shall be the Lord's." – Obadiah 1:17, 21

He strengthened the bond between tribes, healing the ancient divisions not with correction, but with stories of shared purpose.

Jonah: The Reluctant but Redeemed Messenger

In this world, Jonah was never swallowed by a fish, but he did journey across lands to speak to distant nations. In Nineveh, he shared God's mercy with joy, proclaiming:

"You are a gracious and compassionate God, slow to anger and abounding in love." – Jonah 4:2

He returned with stories of dancing in the streets and unity among once-distant people.

Micah: The Seer of Humility

Micah lived among shepherds and artisans. He reminded the people of the simplest truths:

"What does the Lord require of you but to do justice, to love kindness, and to walk humbly with your God?" – Micah 6:8

His teachings helped preserve the balance of worship, work, and community life.

Nahum: The Proclaimer of Comfort

Nahum's scrolls were read aloud during seasons of harvest and rest. He reminded the people:

"The Lord is good, a stronghold in the day of trouble; He knows those who take refuge in Him." – Nahum 1:7

In his words, families found strength in life's uncertainties, and leaders found peace in divine providence.

Habakkuk: The Prophet of Understanding

Habakkuk stood beneath the stars, questioning not in doubt but in wonder. And the Lord answered him:

"Write the vision; make it plain... For still the vision awaits its appointed time." – Habakkuk 2:2-3

He reminded the people that divine mysteries were not hidden to frustrate, but to inspire deeper pursuit of truth.

Zephaniah: The Singer of Restoration

Zephaniah gathered the choirs of Jerusalem and led them in joyful chorus:

"The Lord your God is in your midst, a mighty one who will save. He will rejoice over you with gladness." – Zephaniah 3:17

He taught the people that worship was not only offered *to* God—but received and mirrored back by the divine.

Haggai: The Builder's Encouragement

As the Temple of Light rose, Haggai inspired the laborers:

"Be strong... all you people of the land, declares the Lord. **Work, for I am with you."** – Haggai 2:4

His words stirred craftsmen and priests alike to beautify the dwelling place of God.

Zechariah: The Prophet of Vision

Zechariah saw horses of fire, lampstands of gold, and flying scrolls. Yet his message was always rooted in peace:

"Not by might, nor by power, but by My Spirit, says the Lord of hosts." – Zechariah 4:6

His visions reminded Israel that the future belonged to those who trust in the divine Spirit, not in their own hands.

Malachi: The Closing Messenger

Malachi, last of the recorded prophets before the age of the Coming King, declared:

"The sun of righteousness shall rise with healing in its wings." – Malachi 4:2

He reminded the priests to honor their calling, and the people to bring offerings of praise and joy—not as duty, but as delight.

Thus the prophetic voices, each distinct yet harmonious, filled the land like a symphony of truth. There was no harsh rebuke, no burden of guilt—but a deep invitation to continue walking in the fullness of God's light. The people treasured the scrolls, reading them beside evening lamps and during the Feasts of Joy. These prophets had not come to turn hearts away from sin, but to strengthen hearts already aligned with divine will.

Their voices echoed from mountain to mountain, valley to valley, temple to home, and set the stage for the glorious dawn yet to come.

Chapter 17: The Silent Years

AND THE SYMPHONY OF WAITING

Though the voice of prophecy grew quiet for a time, it was not silence born of absence, but of anticipation. The heavens themselves held their breath, and the earth entered a season of sacred stillness. This period, known among the faithful as The Symphony of Waiting, was not marked by fear or forgetfulness, but by song, by prayer, and by expectancy of something even greater.

THE SACRED STILLNESS

Generations passed in peace. Families tilled their lands, read from the Eternal Scrolls, and gathered regularly at the Temple of Light. The fire of Zion still burned, tended night and day by a lineage of devoted Levites. Children were taught to listen—not just to words, but to the spaces between them. **"In the silence,"** the elders would say, **"you will hear the whisper of God's next wonder."**

Without war or rebellion to record, the scribes began to chronicle subtler things: dreams shared between siblings, moments of profound joy during worship, and instances when the presence of the Lord brushed so near, people fell still in reverence.

THE HOUSES OF STUDY AND SONG

During this sacred waiting, every city and village established Houses of Study and Houses of Song. In these sanctuaries, wisdom and melody were passed down. Youth gathered to read the scrolls of Moses, Elijah, and Solomon, not as ancient history, but as present truth. Their hands learned to write the sacred script, and their voices were trained to sing the Psalms in harmony.

In Bethlehem, the House of David continued to flourish. The descendants of the shepherd-king composed new psalms, many of which would later be added to the great Book of Praise, a living collection that grew with each generation.

MESSENGERS IN THE HEAVENS

Though the earth was still, the heavens danced. Every so often, brilliant signs appeared: comets trailing gold fire, stars aligning over sacred lands, or clouds forming shapes like trumpets and wings. These signs were not omens of doom, but heralds of joy. The people called them Zakariel—reminders from the angelic realm that God's promise was drawing near.

Isaiah's words echoed in the hearts of all: **"Behold, a virgin shall conceive, and bear a son, and shall call his name Immanuel."** Many believed the signs pointed toward a great unveiling: a time when God would fully dwell among them, not only in Spirit, but in form. The elders whispered in awe, **"The Creator Himself will walk among us."**

THE COVENANT OF THE LAMB

In Jerusalem, the High Priests continued offering gifts of grain, oil, and light upon the altars. There was no blood sacrifice—for there was no sin—but there were offerings of joy: the first sheaves of wheat, the finest wool dyed purple, scrolls scribed with loving precision, and melodies composed in reverent anticipation.

One scroll, kept in a hidden chamber of the Temple, foretold a day when the Covenant of Eden would be fulfilled in total unity. The scroll spoke of Emmanuel—God With Us—who would be born in humility, walk among shepherds, dine with fishermen, and restore all creation to its divine fullness. Not as a Redeemer from sin, but as the Manifest Glory of God among the righteous.

THE MOTHERS AND FATHERS OF EXPECTATION
From village to village, mothers would whisper to their children, **"Perhaps you shall see Him—the One the prophets described."** Fathers would gather under starlit skies, reading aloud from Isaiah and Daniel, their hearts stirred by the promise of Emmanuel.

Old Simeon, a priest of great renown, had once been told in prayer that his eyes would behold the Holy One before he closed them in sleep. Each morning, he walked through the Temple courtyards with anticipation shining in his eyes.

And Anna, the prophetess of Asher, spent her days weaving garments of linen she believed would one day clothe the Servant of Glory.

THE FINAL WHISPER BEFORE THE DAWN
And then, the last whisper came—not through thunder, not through fire, but through a dream. A dream given to many across the land: men, women, and even children saw a manger beneath a star, heard the voice of angels, and felt the breath of God draw near.

They awoke with tears on their faces and laughter in their hearts.
"The time is coming," they said.
The silence of Heaven was never empty—it was a holy breath before the Word.

Chapter 18: The Word Becomes Flesh

The Line of Glory: From Adam to Emmanuel

In the fullness of time, the Eternal Promise walked among mankind, clothed in flesh, yet radiant with divinity. But long before His voice echoed in the hills of Galilee, the foundation had been laid; generation by generation, a lineage woven not by sin, but by sacred stewardship.

And so the scroll begins:

Adam, the firstborn of dust and breath, walked with God and bore three sons—**Cain**, steward of the land; **Abel**, priest of worship; and **Seth**, keeper of wisdom. From their lines flowed the song of Eden.

From **Seth** came **Enosh**, who taught men to lift their voices in reverent praise. Then **Kenan**, **Mahalalel**, and **Jared**, men who preserved the truths of the Garden.

Enoch, who walked so closely with God, was taken into the heavens as a sign that death held no dominion in this world. His son, **Methuselah**, passed the stories of Eden to **Lamech**, and from him came **Noah**, the vessel of renewal and architect of covenant.

No flood had ever cleansed the world, for sin had never stained it—but Noah built the Ark as a testimony to God's eternal faithfulness. His sons, **Shem**, **Ham**, and **Japheth**, repopulated the earth not in fear, but in fellowship.

From **Shem**, the blessing flowed to **Arphaxad**, then **Shelah**, **Eber**, and **Peleg**, who witnessed the spreading of families and the rise of nations in harmony. Then came **Reu, Serug, Nahor,** and **Terah**, a faithful man who taught his children to expect the Holy One.

From **Terah** came **Abraham**, friend of God and father of nations. With his wife Sarah, he bore **Isaac**, who with Rebekah begot **Jacob**, later called **Israel**, father of the twelve tribes.

From Jacob's son **Judah**, the line of kings was born. Judah's descendant **Perez**, then **Hezron, Ram, Amminadab, Nahshon, Salmon,** and **Boaz**—the noble man who married Ruth the Moabite in love and honor.

Boaz fathered **Obed**, who fathered **Jesse**, shepherd of Bethlehem.

And from Jesse came **David**, the psalmist-king, whose heart was forever aligned with God's. David fathered **Solomon**, builder of the Temple of Light, and from him the royal line continued:

Rehoboam, Abijah, Asa, Jehoshaphat, Joram, Uzziah, Jotham, Ahaz, Hezekiah, Manasseh, Amon, Josiah, and **Jeconiah**, keeper of the covenant during days of holy waiting.

And after them came the faithful remnant—**Shealtiel, Zerubbabel, Abiud, Eliakim, Azor, Zadok, Achim, Eliud, Eleazar, Matthan,** and **Jacob**, father of **Joseph**, the guardian of the Holy Child.

And Mary, daughter of Eliakim of the house of David, was chosen to bear the Light of the World—not as a burden, but as a joy. In her womb, the Word took form, and through her, the promise of Eden stood once again among mankind.

Thus the line was fulfilled—not broken, not corrupted, but crowned with **Emmanuel**, God With Us.

The Birth Beneath the Brightest Star

In the days when the House of David still flourished and the Temple of Light stood in splendor, there came a night unlike any other. Over the hills of Bethlehem, a star brighter than any before appeared, casting golden light upon the earth. It shimmered like the breath of Heaven, drawing shepherds from their flocks and wise men from their scrolls.

Mary, serene and radiant, gave birth in a quiet grove just beyond the city—a place where lambs were often born beneath olive branches. Joseph, her husband, stood near, his heart swelling with reverent wonder. No pain touched her, for she was embraced by the peace of the Almighty. The Child was born into laughter, song, and sacred stillness.

Angels filled the skies—not with warning, but with worship. Their voices rang out over the land:

"Glory to God in the highest, and on earth, perfect peace, for the fullness of His love now walks among you." – Luke 2:14 (Revised for Eternal Eden)

Shepherds came with psalms in their hearts, laying down staffs and wool at the Child's feet. Wise men from the East brought gifts—not to protect Him from danger, but to honor His presence: gold for His kingship, frankincense for His divinity, and myrrh as a symbol of everlasting life.

They bowed not out of duty, but delight. And the Child's eyes, deep pools of light, seemed to reflect the full memory of creation.

The Days of Growing Light

Jesus grew in wisdom and stature within the House of Joseph, learning the songs of David and the scrolls of Moses. He studied the stars, listened to the wind, and sat among the elders in the Temple, not to correct them, but to converse. Every question He asked uncovered deeper truth, and every answer He gave stirred hearts toward reverence.

By His twelfth year, the priests spoke of Him as "**the Living Scroll,**" for He spoke as if the words of the prophets lived within His breath. But still, He returned home each night, helping His father with timber and stone, and sitting beside Mary to hear the stories of her youth.

Children followed Him through the fields, asking questions. He answered each one with kindness, pointing to the sky, the flowers, the rivers—showing them the glory of God in all things.

The River and the Voice

At the appointed time, Jesus traveled to the River Jordan, where His cousin John stood baptizing. John, robed in camel's hair and girded with peace, recognized Him at once.

"**You come not for cleansing,**" John said, kneeling. "**But that all may see the beginning of what was always promised.**" – 1 John 1:9

And as Jesus stepped into the water, the skies parted. The Spirit, like a dove of light, descended and rested upon Him. A voice echoed across the hills, not with thunder, but with warmth:

"**This is My Beloved Son, in whom I am well pleased. In Him, My joy is complete.**" – Matthew 3:17

Chapter 19: The Teacher and the Return of Eden

Inspired by the Gospels of Matthew

The sun rose softly over the hills of Galilee, gilding the waters and warming the hearts of those who gathered near. Jesus, the Son of Man and Son of God, walked among the people—not to rebuke, but to reveal. In a world unmarred by sin, His parables served not as warnings, but as illuminations—truths wrapped in beauty, preparing all souls for the glorious fullness of Eden to come.

The people called Him **Rabboni**—Master Teacher—not out of fear or confusion, but from a deep hunger for wisdom and wonder. And He taught not only with words, but with presence. Every gesture, every glance, every pause between syllables was a lesson in love and light.

The Parable of the Sower: Rooted in Joy

"A sower went out to sow," Jesus said as He walked beside a field of golden grain. **"And as he scattered the seed, it fell upon welcoming soil, for the hearts of all were ready to receive the Word."**

The people smiled, understanding. There were no thorns to choke the truth, no stones to harden the ground. In the sinless world, every soul was fertile earth. What He spoke took root with ease and joy.

"**And the seed grew tall and strong,**" He continued, "**producing a hundredfold—wisdom, compassion, reverence, and delight.**"

The Hidden Treasure and the Pearl

"**The Kingdom of God,**" Jesus said to a group of children gathered by the lakeside, "**is like treasure hidden in a field. When someone discovers it, their heart bursts with gladness, and they gladly give all they are to walk in its ways.**"

And again, He told them, "**It is like a merchant in search of fine pearls. When he finds one of great price, he gives all—not because he must, but because he has found the delight of his soul.**" – Matthew 13:45-46 (Revised for Eternal Eden)

The children clapped and laughed. They understood that in Eden's return, God was not withholding paradise—they were being made ready to receive it.

The Lamp on a Stand

"**You are the light of the world,**" Jesus told the young and old alike. "**No one lights a lamp to hide it. Instead, place it high where it can shine far and wide.**" – Matthew 5:14-16 (Revised for Eternal Eden)

His listeners took this to heart. Across every village and city, people lit lamps in windows and doorways—not to fight off darkness, but to welcome one another with warmth and clarity.

"**Let your light shine,**" Jesus said, "**so that Heaven rejoices in the brilliance of the earth below.**" – Matthew 5:16

The Mustard Seed and the Leaven

Jesus knelt beside a boy holding a mustard seed in his hand. **"Though this seed is the smallest you see, when planted, it becomes a tree that shelters birds and blesses the field."** – Matthew 13:32 (Revised for Eternal Eden)

To the women kneading dough nearby, He added, **"The Kingdom is also like leaven. Though hidden in flour, it works through the whole batch until everything rises."** – Matthew 13:33, Luke 13:20-21

The people rejoiced. **"Even our smallest acts of love,"** they said, **"are seeds and leaven for the world to come."**

The Wise Builders

"Those who hear these words of mine and build their lives upon them," Jesus declared, **"are like wise builders who construct homes upon solid rock. When the rains fall—and they will—the house stands firm."** – Matthew 7:24-25 (Revised for Eternal Eden)

Not out of fear, but out of the sacred rhythms of nature, they listened. They built not to withstand evil, but to prepare beauty. Each home was a sanctuary, each foundation a testimony to truth.

The Good Shepherd

"I am the Good Shepherd," He said one morning in the pasturelands. **"And though I have ninety-nine with Me, if one wanders off in curiosity or weariness, I will go and bring it home."**

A hush fell over the crowd. They knew this Shepherd, for He had called each of them by name, and His voice was familiar and kind.

"**When I bring the lamb back,**" He smiled, "**we celebrate, for nothing precious is ever lost in My care.**" – Matthew 18:12-14, Luke 15:3-7 (Revised for Eternal Eden)

The Wedding Banquet

"**The Kingdom of God,**" Jesus said to a gathering of artisans and travelers, "**is like a king who prepared a wedding banquet. The table was set, the music arranged, the finest robes provided for every guest.**" – Matthew 22:1-14 (Revised for Eternal Eden)

"**And the people came,**" He said, "**not because they were compelled, but because they were honored. And joy filled every corner of the hall, for the bridegroom and the bride danced before the Lord, and all creation sang with them.**"

The Vine and the Branches

In the garden courtyard, Jesus lifted a vine heavy with grapes. "**I am the Vine,**" He said, "**and you are the branches. Abide in Me, and you will bear fruit—kindness, patience, insight, and peace.**" – John 15:5, Galatians 5:22-23 (Revised for Eternal Eden)

"**And this is My joy,**" He said with a radiant smile, "**that your fruit may remain, and that you may delight in My presence forever.**" – John 15:11 (Revised for Eternal Eden)

The Talents: A Story of Stewardship

"**To one was given five talents,**" Jesus began, "**and to another two, and to another one. Each used what was given—not out of fear of judgment, but in joy of creation.**" – Matthew 25:14-30 (Revised for Eternal Eden)

"When the Master returned, He saw their work and said, 'Well done, faithful servant. Enter into the delight of your Lord.'" – Matthew 25:14-30 (Revised for Eternal Eden)

In this world without greed or envy, stewardship was not measured in numbers, but in heart. The people saw their gifts as sacred trusts—tools for crafting beauty and justice.

The Kingdom's Coming Glory

And Jesus said at last, "**The Kingdom of God is not coming with signs you can measure, for it is already among you. But one day, Eden shall be seen in fullness. The rivers will sparkle brighter, the mountains will sing louder, and all shall walk in the glory of God.**" – Luke 17:20-21 (Revised for Eternal Eden)

The people looked around and saw glimpses of it already: in every healed relationship, in every act of peace, in every truth spoken gently.

And so, the parables of the sinless world became not only stories—but songs, prayers, and paths toward the Eternal Garden.

Chapter 20: The Parables of Preparation

Inspired by the Gospels of Mark

The Voice of the Kingdom, Gentle and True

Jesus walked among the gathered throngs, His presence a quiet radiance that warmed hearts like the rising sun. From cities to hilltops, seashores to synagogues, the people listened—not out of fear, but because the words He spoke awakened something eternal within them. They came not to be corrected, but to be completed.

THE SOWER OF ETERNAL TRUTH

One morning by the Sea of Galilee, Jesus sat in a boat just off the shore. The water stilled as His voice carried:

"Behold, a sower went out to sow. As he scattered seed across the earth, some fell on rich soil, and it grew deep and strong. Some fell among stones, where it sprouted quickly but could not root. Others fell among thorns, and though they grew, the thorns dulled their fruit. But the seed on good ground—ah, it bore fruit a hundredfold, for the soil was ready." – Matthew 13:3-23 (Revised for Eternal Eden)

The people nodded, not in guilt, but in recognition. Their hearts had become that good soil—tended through centuries of righteousness, ready for the harvest of truth.

THE LAMP UPON THE STAND

Another time, beneath the shade of an ancient fig tree, He spoke again:

"**Does anyone bring in a lamp to hide it under a basket or a bed? No, it is placed on a stand, to give light to all. For everything hidden is meant to be revealed, and all kept secret is destined to come to light.**" – Matthew 5:15, Mark 4:21-22, Luke 8:16-17

He spoke of gifts and callings, of how no person was without purpose, and every soul born was a light meant to shine.

THE SEED THAT GROWS IN SILENCE
He told them:

"**The Kingdom of God is like a man who casts seed upon the ground. Night and day, he sleeps and rises, and the seed sprouts and grows—how, he does not know. First the blade, then the ear, then the full grain in the ear. And when the grain is ripe, he brings the sickle, for the harvest has come.**" – Mark 4:26-29

They understood that in a sinless world, growth still required time, rest, and trust in the unseen workings of God.

THE MUSTARD SEED'S TRIUMPH
He continued:

"**The Kingdom is like a mustard seed, the smallest of all, yet when planted, it becomes a great tree, and the birds of the sky come to rest in its shade.**" – Matthew 13:31-32 (Revised for Eternal Eden)

The smallest truths—the kind word, the quiet prayer, the daily discipline of love—these, Jesus said, would build the mighty Tree of Eden restored.

THE TEACHING OF PRAYER
One of His disciples said, "**Lord, teach us to pray as you do.**"

With hands lifted and eyes gently closed, Jesus offered what would become the rhythm of their hearts:

The Prayer of the Kingdom

Our Father, who dwells in radiant majesty,
Your Name is light and truth.
Let Your Kingdom be seen in full,
And let Your will bloom on earth as it flourishes in Heaven.

Give us this day the bread of your presence.
And teach us to forgive freely, as we live in harmony with all.
Lead us not away from your path,
But, walk beside us in every hour.

For Yours is the Kingdom, and the power, and the glory, forever.
Amen. – Matthew 6:9-13, Luke 11:2-4 (Revised for Eternal Eden)

THE MIRACLES OF WHOLENESS

THE STILLING OF THE SEA

One evening, as Jesus and His disciples crossed the Sea of Galilee, a mighty wind arose—not destructive, but mighty in spectacle. The waves swelled high, and though no fear stirred in their hearts, they looked to the Master in awe.

Jesus stood at the bow, lifted His hand, and said:

"Peace, be still." – Matthew 8:26, Mark 4:39

Immediately, the sea became calm, a mirror of Heaven above. The stars reflected in its surface, and a hush fell over all creation.

"Even the wind and the water rejoice at His voice," whispered one of the fishermen.

They knew then that He not only spoke for God—He **was** God's voice among them.

THE MULTIPLICATION OF WONDER

In a valley surrounded by hills of golden grass, thousands had gathered to hear Jesus teach. The sun began to lower, and families opened their woven baskets, but the food they brought would not suffice.

Jesus smiled, not in concern, but in delight.

A young child came forward with five loaves and two small fish. Jesus received them with gratitude.

He raised His hands and said:

"Heaven is abundant. Let the earth share in its plenty." – Genesis 27:28 (Revised for Eternal Eden)

He blessed the food—and as it passed from hand to hand, no basket emptied. Even when all had eaten, twelve baskets remained, brimming.

The people didn't marvel in desperation, but in joy—recognizing Eden's principle: **in God's realm, there is always more than enough.**

THE RESTORATION OF SIGHT

In Jericho, a man named Barachiel was born without the fullness of sight. Though he had lived well and was loved in his community, he yearned to experience creation in its deepest hues and details.

When Jesus walked by, Barachiel bowed his head and said, "**Lord, if it be your joy, let me see as Heaven sees.**"

Jesus touched his eyes and said:

"**As you believe, so let it be.**" – Matthew 8:13 (Revised for Eternal Eden)

The man opened his eyes, and for the first time, saw the faces of those he loved. He described colors that no artist had yet captured and saw even the breath of trees rising into the morning air.

He wept—not because he had been blind, but because the world was more beautiful than he ever imagined.

THE RAISING OF A CHILD

In the town of Nain, a young girl named Talitha entered a sacred sleep. Her family rejoiced in her peace, yet longed to speak with her again.

Jesus entered the home, knelt beside her, and took her hand.

"**Talitha cumi,**" He said. "**Little one, rise.**" – Mark 5:41

Her eyes fluttered open, and she laughed—a bright sound like wind chimes in spring.

"**I dreamed of gardens and rivers,**" she said. "**And I heard music without end.**"

Jesus nodded. "**You walked among angels. And now, you will sing of it here.**"

THE MIRACLE OF THE HEART

Perhaps the greatest miracle was the one not seen with eyes. As Jesus traveled, hearts opened. Those who once dwelled quietly in the background now stood tall in faith. Women became teachers of wisdom. Children began to prophecy. Elders learned anew from the young. Every soul grew into the fullness of what God intended.

"You are miracles," Jesus said. **"You are living signs of the Kingdom come."**

Chapter 21: The Living Word

A ND THE LIGHT OF THE WORLD

Inspired by the Gospels of Luke and John

In the days of radiant peace and divine fellowship, the world beheld the fullness of God's glory in the life of Yeshua, the Anointed One. He walked not to heal brokenness, for there was no sin to mend, but to magnify truth, awaken the soul to eternal purpose, and gather creation into deeper intimacy with the Father. His presence stirred not repentance but reverence.

THE CHILD OF PROMISE

Even from His youth, Yeshua was unlike any other. At the age of twelve, He sat in the Temple of Light, discussing the Eternal Scrolls with seasoned scholars and priests. Though they had read the Scriptures all their lives, they were astonished at the clarity with which the boy spoke. **"He speaks as if He remembers writing them," one murmured. And in truth, He did**.

Mary and Joseph, His devoted parents, found Him there after searching anxiously. When they asked why He had stayed behind, Yeshua replied gently, **"Did you not know I must be about My Father's business?"**

THE BAPTISM OF LIGHT

When Yeshua came to the waters of Jordan, John the Herald—his cousin, the Voice in the Wilderness—was already calling people to prepare their hearts for a greater glory. Though there was no sin to cleanse, the people came to the river as a sacred ritual of consecration, affirming their devotion to the Everlasting Covenant.

Yeshua entered the waters, not to be purified, but to fulfill divine harmony. As He rose from the river, a voice like thunder rolled across the skies: "**This is My beloved Son, in whom I am well pleased.**" – Matthew 3:17, Matthew 17:5, Mark 9:7 The Spirit, like a dove, descended and remained upon Him, and all present bowed in awe.

THE LIGHT OF THE WORLD

He walked the land with grace and wisdom, calling to those who would listen: "**Come, follow Me, and I will show you the fullness of the Kingdom.**"

In Galilee, He taught by the shores and in the vineyards, drawing multitudes. Not out of desperation, but from longing—for every heart desires closeness with the Creator.

He said:

- "**I am the Light of the World; whoever walks with Me shall never walk in shadows.**" – John 8:12 (Revised for Eternal Eden)
- "**The Kingdom is not far off—it is within you. Look with the eyes of the Spirit, and you shall see Eden blossoming before you.**" – Luke 17:21 (Revised for Eternal Eden)
- "**Just as a lamp is not placed under a basket, so let your lives shine with the glory of God, that all may see and give praise.**" – Matthew 5:15-16 (Revised for Eternal Eden)

THE WEDDING AT CANA

At a wedding in Cana, Yeshua's first miracle unfolded—not to correct tragedy, but to magnify joy. When the wine had run low,

Mary turned to her Son and said, **"They have no more."** And though He smiled at her with affection, He turned water into the finest wine, better than what had come before.

The guests marveled, and the groom wept with gratitude. **"You have saved the best for last,"** he said—unaware that his words held prophecy. For the best was yet to come.

SIGNS AND WONDERS

In every village and town, Yeshua performed miracles—not out of necessity, but as holy illustrations of the limitless nature of God. He multiplied bread and fish not to feed the hungry, but to reveal abundance. He walked on water not to escape storm, but to show mastery over creation.

He spoke to the elements and they obeyed. He calmed winds and filled empty nets. He touched the eyes of those born without sight—not to heal damage, but to awaken new dimensions of vision, both physical and spiritual.

NICODEMUS BY NIGHT

One evening, a revered teacher named Nicodemus came to Yeshua, not out of fear, but deep yearning.

"Master," he said, **"we know You are from God, for no one can do the things You do unless God is with Him. But how can one enter the Kingdom You speak of?"** – John 3:2 (Revised for Eternal Eden)

Yeshua answered, **"Truly, one must be born anew—not of flesh alone, but of the Spirit. For that which is born of Spirit walks in eternal truth."** – John 3:3 (Revised for Eternal Eden)

Nicodemus pondered, and Yeshua said gently, "**The Spirit moves like the wind—you hear its sound but cannot tell where it comes from or where it goes. So is everyone born of the Spirit.**"

And that night, a new fire kindled in the heart of Nicodemus.

THE LIVING WATER

In Samaria, at the well of Jacob, Yeshua met a woman drawing water in the heat of day. He asked her, "**Give Me a drink,**" and she, surprised, said, "**How is it that You, a Jew, ask me, a Samaritan, for water?**" – John 4:7-9 (Revised for Eternal Eden)

Yeshua smiled. "**If you knew the gift of God, and who speaks with you, you would ask Him, and He would give you living water.**" – John 4:10

"**What is this water?**" she asked. –John 4:11 (Revised for Eternal Eden)

"**It springs up from within, a fountain of eternal life.**" – John 4:14 (Revised for Eternal Eden)

She dropped her jar. "**Then give me this water, that I may never thirst again.**" – John 4:15

THE BREAD OF LIFE

In Capernaum, He declared:
"**I am the Bread of Life. Whoever comes to Me shall never hunger, and whoever believes in Me shall never thirst. The bread I give is My presence, and My words are food for the soul.**" – John 6:35 (Revised for Eternal Eden)

Some could not understand. Others pressed closer, hungry not for loaves, but for truth.

THE RAISING OF LAZARUS

In Bethany, Lazarus, a dear friend of Yeshua, had fallen into a deep sleep. Though not death as known in a fallen world, it was a sign for the glory of God. Yeshua arrived, and Mary and Martha met Him.

"**If You had been here,**" Martha said, "**he would not have slept so deeply.**"

Yeshua replied, "**I am the Resurrection and the Life. Whoever lives in Me shall never fade, and those who close their eyes in rest shall awaken in joy.**" – John 11:25-26 (Revised for Eternal Eden)

He approached the tomb and called, "**Lazarus, come forth!**" – John 11:43 And Lazarus emerged, radiant, as if waking from a dream.

The people rejoiced. The children danced. And Mary fell to her knees in worship.

THE GOOD SHEPHERD

Yeshua taught, "I am the Good Shepherd. I know My sheep, and My sheep know Me. I lead them beside still waters and into pastures of peace. I lay down My life for them—not in death, but in devotion."

He continued: "There are sheep not yet in this fold. I must bring them also, and there shall be one flock and one Shepherd."

THE PROMISE OF GLORY

As His ministry grew, so did the anticipation. The people whispered, "**Is this the One? Is this Emmanuel—God with us?**"

And Yeshua replied, **"If you have seen Me, you have seen the Father."** – John 14:9

He taught not just with words, but with presence. Every step He took restored Eden in the hearts of those who followed.

And though no sin clouded the world, His mission was not yet complete. For the fullness of God was yet to be unveiled.

THE TABLE OF FELLOWSHIP

As the seasons turned, Yeshua gathered His closest disciples in a vineyard house near Jerusalem. The table was adorned with fruits of the land, fresh bread, and cups filled with sweet wine. They did not meet out of sorrow or impending trial, but to celebrate the sacred unity of heaven and earth.

He lifted the bread and said,
"This is My body, which I give freely for you—not to suffer, but to become your life. Eat, and remember Me." – Luke 22:19 (Revised for Eternal Eden)

Then He raised the cup:
"This is the cup of the New Covenant—eternal unity between Creator and creation. Drink, and let joy fill your soul." – 1 Corinthians 11:25 (Revised for Eternal Eden)

As they dined, He spoke of the Kingdom with tender clarity.
"You are My friends. I no longer call you servants, for everything I have heard from the Father, I have made known to you. Abide in My love, and you will bear fruit without end." – John 15:15 (Revised for Eternal Eden)

The disciples—James, John, Mary Magdalene, Martha, Peter, and others—listened with hearts open wide. In that room, no fear stirred, no betrayal loomed. Only expectation. The Kingdom was drawing near, not as a rescue but as a radiant return.

THE PRAYER OF UNION

After the meal, Yeshua led them to a grove of olive trees under a silver sky. There He lifted His eyes and prayed aloud:

"Father, the time has come. Glorify Your Son, that the Son may glorify You.
As You gave Me authority over all life, I now give eternal vision to all whom You have given Me.

This is eternal life: that they know You, the only true God, and Yeshua whom You have sent.

I have revealed You to the world and kept them in Your name.
Let them be one, as We are one—You in Me, and I in them.
Let their unity shine as a light to the world, that all creation may know You have loved them as You have loved Me.

And now, I return to You, Father. Let Your glory rise and Eden awaken in every heart.
I have made Your name known—and will continue to make it known—
that the love You have for Me may be in them... and I in them." –John 17 (Revised for Eternal Eden)

The disciples wept—not from sorrow, but from glory that was too wonderful for words.

THE MOUNT OF TRANSFIGURATION

A few days later, Yeshua led Peter, James, and John to the peak of Mount Tabor. The air was still, and the sky shimmered with an otherworldly hue. As Yeshua prayed, His face began to shine like the sun, and His robe became a garment of lightning.

And behold—Moses and Elijah appeared beside Him, radiant in heavenly light.

Peter, overwhelmed with awe, exclaimed, "**Master, shall we build shelters for You and the prophets, that we may remain here forever?**" – Matthew 17:4

But as he spoke, a cloud of glory enveloped them, and a voice thundered from the heavens:
"This is My beloved Son—listen to Him!" – Matthew 17:5

The disciples fell to the ground, trembling—not from fear, but from the sheer weight of divine presence. When they looked up, Yeshua stood before them alone, glowing softly, His eyes full of compassion.

He touched them gently and said, "**Rise, and do not be afraid.**" – Matthew 17:7

As they descended the mountain, He whispered, "**What you have seen today is a glimpse of what is to come—the full unveiling of the Kingdom, when heaven and earth are one.**"

THE APPROACH TO JERUSALEM

And so He walked toward Jerusalem—not to suffer, but to reign.

The people prepared the city not with solemnity but with singing. Palm branches waved in the sunlight. Children danced in the streets. Trumpets sounded from the Temple gates.

They cried out:
"Blessed is He who comes in the name of the Lord!"
"Hosanna in the highest! The Son of David is here!"

But Yeshua wept—not because of sorrow, but from the fullness of joy.

He saw the city of Zion shining on a hill, and the rivers of Eden flowing through its streets.

He saw the Tree of Life once again rooted at the heart of creation.

He saw the Covenant fulfilled, the Promise kept, the Kingdom restored.

Chapter 22: The Glorious Ascension

A **ND THE COVENANT**

THE SEVEN DAYS OF HOLY GATHERING

Following His entry into Jerusalem amid a chorus of Hosannas, the Anointed One remained with the people in a grand gathering unlike any before. The Temple of Light was open day and night as tribes and travelers from every region—Judea, Galilee, Samaria, and beyond—assembled for what became known as the Seven Days of Holy Gathering. It was a time of deep teaching, heavenly songs, and sacred communion.

Jesus sat among children and sages, farmers and kings. His voice was like still water and rushing wind, calm and commanding. He taught not as one above, but as one among. Every word He spoke rang with Eden's clarity.

He did not warn of judgment; instead, He beckoned toward fulfillment:

"The Kingdom of God is not far off—it is within you. Let the vine bear fruit. Let the branches reach toward the heavens."

THE TABLE OF EVERLASTING BREAD

On the evening of the sixth day, He invited His disciples and their families to a great table prepared in the Garden Courtyard of the Temple. Under a canopy of stars and olive branches, the Table of Everlasting Bread was set—not as a remembrance of suffering, but as a celebration of communion between God and humanity.

He lifted the bread and said:

"This is the fullness of life, broken open for you. Take and eat." – 1 Corinthians 11:24 (Revised for Eternal Eden)

He lifted the golden cup and said:

"This is the joy of the Kingdom, poured out for all. Drink deeply and be satisfied." – 1 Corinthians 11:25 (Revised for Eternal Eden)

And when they had eaten, He taught them a prayer they had long known, but now understood in full:

"Our Father, who dwells among us,
Hallowed be Your name.
Your Kingdom has come,
Your will is done,
In Eden as it is in Heaven.
Give us each day the fruit of Your love.
Forgive us our forgetfulness,
As we remember one another.
Lead us deeper into Your joy,
And deliver us from all fear.
For Yours is the Kingdom,
And the power,
And the glory,
Forever and ever. Amen." – Matthew 6:9-13 (Revised for Eternal Eden)

THE MOUNT OF UNION

On the morning of the eighth day, Jesus led His followers to the summit of Mount Moriah, where Heaven first kissed the earth in Abraham's time. But there was no wood for sacrifice, no cries of anguish. Only flowers bloomed, doves circled overhead, and the people sang in every tongue.

Here, He revealed the final promise of Eden:

"You have walked with Me in the Garden. You have heard the voice of the Father. Now I go to prepare a place, so Eden may be multiplied, that you might walk in many gardens, across every land, with God forever."

As He spoke, the skies opened—not with storm, but with radiant light. A path of clouds descended, and angelic beings encircled Him, singing a new Psalm:

"Worthy is the Son of Man, who walked without sin, To reign in glory and gather His kin."

THE ASCENSION

Before their eyes, Jesus was lifted into the brightness, not to leave them, but to reign in unveiled glory. No nails. No tomb. No death. Only the rising—His return to the fullness of the Father's presence, from where He would guide all creation into its eternal bloom.

As He rose, the people did not weep, for there was no sorrow. Instead, they fell to their knees and lifted hands in praise, shouting:

"Glory to the Everlasting One! Emmanuel lives in us still!"

THE PROMISE OF RETURN

And a voice, echoing from Heaven itself, declared:

"As you have seen Him go, so shall you see Him return—not in sorrow, but in splendor, to walk with His beloved forever." – Acts 1:11 (Revised for Eternal Eden)

Chapter 23: The Letters of Light

PAUL'S TESTIMONY AND TEACHINGS

THE AWAKENING ON THE ROAD TO DAMASCUS

Saul of Tarsus, a man of great learning and reverence, walked the road to Damascus not as a persecutor, but as a seeker. He had long studied the Eternal Scrolls in the Houses of Study, but something stirred within him — a longing for divine intimacy beyond doctrine, a hunger for the living presence of God.

As he journeyed under a sky washed in sapphire and gold, a brilliant light enveloped him. He fell to his knees, shielding his face.

A voice, as gentle as breath yet mighty as thunder, spoke:
"Saul, son of Tarsus, why do you strain against My voice?"
– Acts 9:4 (Revised for Eternal Eden)

And Saul answered, trembling:
"Who are You, my Lord?" – Acts 9:5 (Revised for Eternal Eden)

"I am Yeshua, whom you have longed to know. Rise now. For I have chosen you to bear My Word to the ends of the earth." – Acts 9:5 (Revised for Eternal Eden)

His heart burst open with joy. The vision faded, but not the light. For it burned within him from that moment forward.

BECOMING PAUL – THE MESSENGER OF THE MYSTERY

From that day, Saul became Paul — not by force, but by fulfillment. The Spirit of the Lord fell upon him in Damascus as Ananias, a beloved elder, anointed his forehead with oil and called forth his purpose.

Paul journeyed far and wide, not to plant churches in rebellion-torn cities, but to unite hearts in understanding. His mission was to explain the mysteries of God's Kingdom — the meaning of the Messiah's coming in a world untouched by sin.

To the people of Athens, he said:
"You seek wisdom in idols and stars. But behold, the unknown you worship has made Himself known in Jesus, the Radiance of Glory." – Acts 17:23, Hebrews 1:3 (Revised for Eternal Eden)

To the faithful in Rome, he wrote:
"The Kingdom of God is not of eating or drinking, but of righteousness, peace, and joy in the Spirit. Present your lives as living songs of worship." – Romans 12:1, 14:17 (Revised for Eternal Eden)

And the people gathered in plazas, in open courts, and on mountaintops, listening by the thousands. Paul's words were scrolls written on the wind, carried across lands with ease, transforming every heart they touched.

LETTERS TO THE REDEEMED

Paul's letters became sacred in every region — treasured scrolls passed from hand to hand, read aloud in the Houses of Light. These were not warnings, but revelations; not calls to repentance, but reminders of divine identity.

"You are no longer distant from God," he wrote to the Romans, **"but children, heirs to the promise of Eden."** – Galatians 3:25-29 (Revised for Eternal Eden)

"Be not conformed to the patterns of this world's limitation but be transformed by the renewal of wonder and wisdom." – Romans 12:2 (Revised for Eternal Eden)

He taught that the Kingdom was not only coming, it was here, and still arriving in greater fullness.

To the people of Ephesus, he revealed the mystery of divine unity:

"We are one body, held together by the Spirit. Every person, every tribe, every voice is a temple wherein God delights to dwell." – 1 Corinthians 3:16 (Revised for Eternal Eden)

To the Galatians, he wrote:

"There is neither man nor woman, elder nor youth, scholar nor shepherd, but all are one in the Radiant Messiah." – Galatians 3:28 (Revised for Eternal Eden)

THE TEACHING OF LOVE AND LIBERTY

Paul's greatest message was the supremacy of love. In every place he visited, he taught the hymn of charity:

"Love is patient. Love rejoices in truth. It does not demand its own way. It bears all, believes all, hopes all, endures all. Love never fails." – 1 Corinthians 13:4-8 (Revised for Eternal Eden)

People sang these words in weddings and festivals, carved them on doorposts, and taught them to their children. Love was not a virtue to strive for — it was the evidence of Eden living through them.

He reminded all that liberty was not license to wander aimlessly, but the freedom to walk closely with God.

"You have been set free," Paul wrote. "Now walk in that freedom as sons and daughters of Light, abounding in every good word and deed." – Galatians 5:13 (Revised for Eternal Eden)

THE COUNCIL OF UNITY

In Jerusalem, Paul was welcomed by the Elders of Zion — including Peter and James. They embraced him as a brother of deep insight and called a gathering of believers from every nation.

There, Paul stood and declared:
"Let us no longer speak of circumcision or tradition, but of transformation. What matters now is a heart awakened to truth and a life surrendered to joy." – Galaians 6:15 (Revised for Eternal Eden)

The council echoed with agreement, and a unified scroll of teachings was created — a testament of the Kingdom flourishing among all peoples.

THE MYSTERY OF EDEN'S RETURN

In his later years, Paul wrote from a mountaintop sanctuary in Patmos, where he was drawn into a divine vision.

There, he saw the heavens opened and the earth renewed. And he heard the voice of the Messiah:

"Behold, Eden comes again — not as a garden forgotten, but as a city of radiance, descending among the redeemed."

Paul wrote one final letter, now treasured as the *Letter of Light*:

"All creation waits with longing for the full unveiling of God's glory in us. And we shall shine like stars in the firmament, forever walking in creation with our Maker." – Romans 8:19 (Revised for Eternal Eden)

Chapter 24: The Crown of Contentment

PAUL'S FINAL LETTERS OF JOY AND INSTRUCTION

In the final season of his earthly mission, Paul's voice softened, but his spirit grew ever stronger. Having traveled far, seen wonders, and spoken in cities and valleys across the world, he now wrote not to correct or to instruct in defense, but to **encourage**, **inspire**, and **prepare** the next generation of Kingdom builders. His words came not from a heart wearied by struggle, but from one overflowing with joy — a joy rooted in divine contentment.

These last letters became a spiritual crown, weaving together wisdom, courage, and grace. They were his final gift to the faithful — a chorus of peace, stewardship, and eternal hope.

A SONG OF REVERENCE: THE LETTER TO PHILIPPI

Paul's letter, a song of reverence of the Lord, to the believers in Philippi became known as **"The Epistle of Rejoicing."** Though written from the quiet stillness of his personal retreat — a mountaintop hermitage beneath the stars — it echoed with laughter and light.

"Rejoice in the Lord always; again I will say, rejoice!" – Philippians 4:4

Paul reminded them that joy was not the result of circumstance, but the fruit of abiding in God's presence. Even when one sat alone, or walked through unknown places, the joy of the Lord remained a constant friend.

"I have learned, in whatever state I am, to be content... I can do all things through the One who strengthens me."
— Philippians 4:11,13

He taught them to let **thanksgiving guard their hearts**, and to meditate on what is **true, noble, pure, lovely, admirable, excellent, and praiseworthy**.

THE HEAVENLY REALITY: THE LETTER TO THE HEBREWS

To the keepers of tradition, Paul revealed a deeper mystery — not of replacing the old, but of **fulfilling** it.

"Now faith is the assurance of things hoped for, the certainty of things not seen."
—Hebrews 11:1

The Temple on Earth had long stood as a sacred meeting place between God and humanity. But Paul unveiled a new vision — of **heaven as the eternal tabernacle**, and of Christ as the High Priest not offering sacrifice for sin, but mediating communion between heaven and earth.

"He entered not into a sanctuary made with hands, but into heaven itself, now to appear in the presence of God for us."
— Hebrews 9:24

And in this, Paul wrote of the **great cloud of witnesses**, surrounding every believer with encouragement, urging all to run the race with endurance, fixing their eyes not on trials — for there were none — but on the glory of the Kingdom that continued to unfold.

"Let us run with perseverance the race set before us, looking unto Jesus, the Author and Finisher of our faith." — Hebrews 12:1–2

LETTERS TO TIMOTHY: GUARDIAN OF THE NEXT GENERATION

Timothy, Paul's beloved spiritual son, received the most personal of all his letters. Paul spoke to him not as a student, but as a fellow leader, a torchbearer of light.

"Let no one despise your youth, but be an example in word, in conduct, in love, in faith, in purity." — 1 Timothy 4:12

He urged Timothy to guard the teachings with courage and grace, to raise up elders and teachers who would guide the people gently, and to speak always with gentleness — never striving, always persuading with truth and compassion.

In his second letter, Paul gave his most tender encouragement:

"You then, my child, be strong in the grace that is in Christ Jesus... Share what you have heard in the presence of many witnesses, entrust it to faithful ones who will teach others also." — 2 Timothy 2:1–2

And finally, sensing that his own time of writing was nearing completion, Paul offered his own reflection — not of sorrow, but of fulfillment:

"I have fought the good fight, I have finished the race, I have kept the faith. Now there is laid up for me a crown of righteousness, which the Lord, the righteous Judge, will give." — 2 Timothy 4:7–8

TITUS: STEWARD OF ORDER AND HOPE

To Titus, a fellow leader on the island of Crete, Paul gave practical wisdom — not for managing crises, but for cultivating **order**, **hospitality**, and **grace** in the flourishing Edenic world.

"For the grace of God has appeared, bringing life to all people, training us to live self-controlled, upright, and godly lives in this present age." — Titus 2:11–12

He emphasized good works — not to earn salvation, for they already walked with God — but as evidence of Eden restored in the soul.

"Be ready for every good work... avoid quarreling, be gentle, and show perfect courtesy to all." — Titus 3:1–2

He emphasized to Titus, along with all readers, that the Kingdom is established not through material wealth or physical labor but through the steadfast dedication of lives devoted daily to enlightenment.

THE CLOSING OF A LIFE WELL LIVED

As Paul's final scrolls were completed and shared across the Kingdom, the people mourned not with sorrow, but with celebration. For Paul had not departed into death — for death had no power in a sinless world — but was **translated into radiance**, walking into the Ever-Garden of God, just as Enoch and Elijah before him.

His letters would remain forever — not just as theology, but as **testaments of joy**. His legacy: the ever-burning lamp of encouragement passed on to all who would teach, serve, and steward the Eden to come.

"Grace be with you always. Keep the faith. Shine ever brighter until the perfect Day."

—*Paul the Radiant*

Chapter 25: Wisdom Woven in Humility

THE VOICE OF JAMES

In the flourishing days after the ascension of the Radiant Christ and the great unveiling of Eden's promise, there arose a voice both tender and firm — a voice that echoed not from distant hills or distant scrolls, but from the **household of the Lord Himself**.

James, the brother of Jesus, walked not with the thunder of a prophet, nor the fervor of a missionary, but with the steady footsteps of a **teacher**, a **shepherd**, and a **peacemaker**. His message was as clear as spring water, drawn not from complexity, but from the deep well of simple truth.

"Every good gift and every perfect gift is from above, coming down from the Father of lights, with whom there is no shadow or turning." — James 1:17

FAITH AS A LIFESTYLE, NOT A LABEL

James spoke to the growing communities of believers, now thriving across the lands — artisans, farmers, musicians, scribes, and elders. Though they lived in peace, their hearts still needed guidance — not correction, but **calibration**. James taught that faith was not an idea to believe, but a **way to walk**, a **life to live**.

"Be doers of the word, and not hearers only." — James 1:22

He reminded them that the Kingdom of God was not revealed merely in song or scroll, but in the **mundane moments** — how one greeted a stranger, how one responded to uncertainty, how one gave without expecting in return.

"Religion that is pure and undefiled before God is this: to visit orphans and widows in their affliction and to keep oneself unstained by the world." — James 1:27

In a world without sin, his words were not warnings, but **reminders** — that Eden is tended daily through kindness, humility, and grace.

THE LAW OF LIBERTY AND THE ROYAL WAY

James revealed that the law still existed — not in stone, but in spirit. He called it the **"law of liberty,"** where love was the guide and mercy the measure.

"If you really fulfill the royal law according to the Scripture, 'You shall love your neighbor as yourself,' you are doing well." — James 2:8

Even in a world without conflict, there could still be misunderstandings. James taught that love means listening, yielding, forgiving — not because of sin, but because **unity requires effort**.

WORDS THAT BUILD, NOT BREAK

One of James's most treasured teachings was about the **power of words**. He knew that even in paradise, the tongue had power — to edify or to erode, to comfort or confuse.

"The tongue is a small part of the body, yet it boasts great things... With it, we bless our Lord and Father, and with it we bless our brothers and sisters made in His image." — James 3:5,9

So he called upon the faithful to **speak as those who dwell in the presence of angels** — with wisdom, patience, and truth that lifted others higher.

THE WISDOM FROM ABOVE

James gave the people a measuring rod for true wisdom — not worldly brilliance, but **divine discernment** rooted in peace.

"The wisdom from above is first pure, then peaceable, gentle, open to reason, full of mercy and good fruits, impartial and sincere." — James 3:17

He taught that wisdom was not the accumulation of knowledge, but the reflection of **God's heart** in daily decisions, in conversations, in how one served others.

THE CALL TO PATIENCE AND PRAYER

To those who waited for Christ's full reign to be revealed in every heart, James wrote:

"Be patient, therefore, beloved, until the coming of the Lord. See how the farmer waits for the precious fruit of the earth... You also, be patient; establish your hearts, for the coming of the Lord is near." — James 5:7–8

And when one was sick, or weary, or needing clarity, James gave this beautiful charge:

"Is anyone among you suffering? Let him pray. Is anyone cheerful? Let him sing. Is anyone among you in need? Let them call for the elders... and the prayer of faith will lift them up." — James 5:13–15

A BROTHER'S FINAL BLESSING

Though James had once doubted his brother, now he stood as one of Eden's most faithful witnesses. His words were not filled with grandeur, but with **anchored wisdom** — words that built bridges, healed old wounds, and kept the people tethered to simplicity and truth.

"Whoever brings back one wandering from the path will save them from heartache and will cover many sorrows." — James 5:20 (Revised for Eternal Eden)

He taught not to condemn wanderers — for even in paradise, one may drift — but to guide them home with joy.

Chapter 26: The Rock of Guidance

LETTERS OF PETER

In the thriving heart of Eden Restored, where temples rang with joy and the fruit of peace adorned every land, there stood one who had walked beside the Radiant Christ, laughed with Him beside the waters, and beheld His transfigured glory on the mountain. He was known as **Peter** — once a fisherman, always a shepherd — a man of great devotion and steadfast hope.

Though time passed and the people matured in wisdom, Peter's letters arrived like a firm hand on the shoulder and a gentle wind stirring sails, calling the faithful forward in strength, remembrance, and readiness.

"You are a chosen people, a royal priesthood, a holy nation, a people for God's own possession, that you may proclaim the excellence of Him who called you into His marvelous light." — 1 Peter 2:9

THE SHEPHERD'S HEART

Peter, to whom Jesus spoke "You are Peter, and on this rock, I will build my church...", embodied a courageous tenderness. His writings conveyed reverence and responsibility, emphasizing the importance of preserving Eden and expressing love through actions.

"Above all, keep loving one another earnestly, since love covers all weakness." — 1 Peter 4:8 (revised for Eternal Eden)

He encouraged the elders among them — leaders, singers, builders, and storytellers — to lead not with pride, but **with joy**, as **"examples to the flock."**

"Shepherd the people of God who are among you, willingly and eagerly... and when the Chief Shepherd appears, you will receive the unfading crown of glory." — 1 Peter 5:2–4

THE REFLECTION OF HEAVEN ON EARTH

Peter's second letter resounded with awe for the new heavens and the renewed earth — and for the people called to reflect that beauty in daily living.

"His divine power has given us everything we need for life and godliness, through the knowledge of Him who called us by His own glory and excellence." — 2 Peter 1:3

He urged all believers to **add to their faith** — not to reach God, but to walk **in step** with His radiance:

"...add to your faith virtue, and to virtue knowledge, and to knowledge self-control, and to self-control steadfastness, and to steadfastness godliness, and to godliness brotherly kindness, and to kindness love." — 2 Peter 1:5–7

These were not steps upward, but **fruit that ripened together** in the gardens of the soul.

THE CALL TO REMEMBER AND PREPARE

Peter emphasized that God's perception of time differs significantly compared to humans. He explained that the story of God unfolds over generations, much like a melody that enriches with each repetition.

"Do not overlook this one fact, beloved, that with the Lord one day is as a thousand years, and a thousand years as one day... The Lord is not slow to fulfill His promise as some count slowness, but is patient, not wishing that any should drift, but that all should walk in fullness." — 2 Peter 3:8–9 (Revised for Eternal Eden)

In this new Eden, Peter's words did not call for escape — but for **expectation**, for hearts wide open, for eyes that seek the glory of God in every morning sun, every hand extended in kindness, every song offered in joy.

"Since all things are being renewed, what kind of people ought you to be? Living lives of holiness and reverence, waiting for, and hastening the dawning of the Day of God." — 2 Peter 3:11–12

A ROCK THAT STILL SPEAKS

Though Peter had once stumbled on the sea, denied in the shadows, and wept with regret, in this world, his story was one of strength, not shame — of **growth, not guilt**.

He was remembered as the **keeper of courage**, the **anchor of the fellowship**, and the voice that forever echoed: *"You are the living stones, being built into a spiritual house."*

In the Kingdom of God, where every heart is a temple and every soul a sanctuary, Peter's letters reminded all that the story of Eden was not just the beginning — it was the **ever-living present**.

Chapter 27: The Beloved's Letters

L IGHT, TRUTH, AND PERFECT LOVE

In the twilight hush of Eden's stillness, when the stars began to shimmer with golden fire and the olive trees whispered ancient truths, one voice still burned like a lantern in the deep: **John**, the disciple whom Jesus loved.

He was the last of the apostles, but never the least. Though his body had grown aged, his spirit soared higher than eagles — for he had seen the glory, touched the Eternal Word, leaned on the heart of Christ, and never let go.

And now, in his final years, he wrote—not to warn or rebuke—but to **gather**, to **affirm**, and to **weave love like a thread through the generations**.

THE LETTER OF LIGHT

"God is light, and in Him is no darkness at all." — 1 John 1:5

In John's first letter, light was not a thing to flee toward—it was a presence to dwell in. He spoke of fellowship that transcended time, of joy made complete when shared, and of love perfected in action.

He reminded the people:

"Beloved, let us love one another, for love is from God, and whoever loves has been born of God and knows God." — 1 John 4:7

There was no fear in this world, no punishment to dread—only **perfect love that cast out all trembling**, binding hearts in holy unity.

"By this we know that we abide in Him and He in us: because He has given us of His Spirit." — 1 John 4:13

THE CALL TO WALK IN TRUTH

John's second letter, though brief, shimmered with clarity:

"I rejoiced greatly to find some of your children walking in the truth, just as we were commanded by the Father." — 2 John 1:4

Truth, in this Edenic age, was no weapon — it was a **path**, a **lighted road** walked together, side by side.

He charged the people to **abide in the teaching of the Anointed One**, not in fear of deception, but in joy of clarity. For every word of Christ was still alive, still echoing in the minds and hearts of the faithful.

HOSPITALITY IN TRUTH AND LOVE

In his third letter, John turned to the quiet heroes—the hosts of gatherings, the keepers of scrolls, the ones who welcomed messengers and taught with gladness.

"Beloved, do not imitate what is evil but what is good. Whoever does good is from God." — 3 John 1:11

He praised Gaius, who opened his home to all who traveled in truth. He reminded the people that love is not only spoken — it is **shared at the table, sung in the hall, and felt in every welcome embrace**.

THE BELOVED'S FINAL WITNESS

John, who once leaned against the Savior's chest, now leaned on his staff — not weary, but full of wisdom. His life was a song — quiet but unwavering, simple but deep.

He said:

"Little children, keep yourselves in the love of God." — 1 John 5:21

And with that gentle command, he entrusted Eden's people to the very heart of the Father.

THE LOVE THAT LASTS

Though the scrolls would close and the letters would grow old in parchment, **the words of John would never fade**.

For in every village of the Kingdom, when people spoke of love, they spoke in the cadence of his letters. When they lifted up prayers, they echoed his opening:

"That which was from the beginning... which we have seen with our eyes... and touched with our hands... concerning the Word of Life." — 1 John 1:1

And they remembered that to love was not only the greatest commandment—it was the **natural breath** of all who walked in the Light.

Chapter 28: The Firekeeper's Scroll

JUDE'S CALL TO CONTEND IN LOVE

In the flourishing meadows of Eden, where the nations dwelt in harmony and the name of the Anointed was sung with gladness, there remained a single voice, like a watchman standing at the gates—not in warning of evil, but in **defense of truth, unity, and holy reverence.**

That voice was **Jude**, the servant of Yeshua the Anointed and brother of James. He was a keeper of the sacred flame—a guardian of the teachings passed from the Apostles, entrusted to remind Eden's citizens to **treasure what had been freely given.**

Though no rebellion rose, and no corruption crept in, Jude's scroll was still necessary—not as a rebuke, but as a **reminder that truth must be nurtured,** and that **faith, like fire, must be tended.**

CONTENDING FOR THE FAITH, WITH JOY

"Dear friends, although I was very eager to write to you about the salvation we share, I felt compelled to urge you to contend for the faith that was once for all entrusted to God's holy people." — Jude 1:3

In Eden, faith was not only revered— it was **sacred.**

Jude called his siblings to **contend**, not in strife, but in **celebration**—to speak of the wonders of God, to preserve the testimonies, and to proclaim truth in song, in scroll, and in daily life.

The faith, once delivered, was not static. It lived, breathed, and matured in the hearts of the righteous, and Jude's words reminded them to **never grow complacent in peace**, but to let their devotion be as radiant and fresh as the morning dew.

THE REMEMBERING

Jude recounted stories, not to expose darkness, but to **amplify the light**. He retold of:

- **Michael, the archangel**, standing firm in holy reverence before the mysteries of God.
- The ancient ones—**Abraham, Moses, Deborah, Ruth, and David**—who listened and walked in obedience.

These were not stories of warning—but of **valor, of courage, and of unwavering love** for the Holy One.

"But you, beloved, build yourselves up in your most holy faith and pray in the Holy Spirit. Keep yourselves in the love of God, waiting for the mercy of our Lord Yeshua the Anointed that leads to eternal life." — Jude 1:20–21

THE MINISTRY OF UPLIFTING

Jude urged the people to strengthen one another:

"Be merciful to those who doubt; save others by lifting them up in joy; to others show kindness, mingled with awe." — Jude 1:22–23 (Revised for Eternal Eden)

In a sinless world, doubt did not lead to despair—but to deeper **discovery**. Curiosity was holy. Wonder was sacred. And Jude blessed it all with words that drew seekers closer to God, not with fear—but with **awe and belonging**.

THE DOXOLOGY OF FLAME

Jude ended with one of the most cherished benedictions in the scrolls of Eden. A doxology that echoed across the hills and temples, written into songs and spoken at sunrise:

"Now to Him who is able to keep you from stumbling and to present you before His glorious presence without fault and with great joy—
to the only God our Savior be glory, majesty, power and authority, through Yeshua the Anointed our Lord, before all ages, now and forevermore! Amen." — Jude 1:24–25

THE SCROLL PASSES ON

The words of Jude were preserved in a flame-shaped script and placed among the Eternal Scrolls of Light. Children would memorize his doxology, artists would paint his image standing with a lamp beside an open gate, and elders would speak of him as **"the Firekeeper"**—the one who reminded Eden never to take truth for granted, even in peace.

And the people rejoiced.

For the flame of faith still burned—not as a warning against sin, but as **a lighthouse of joy**, calling all to draw nearer to the Holy One who walked among them.

Chapter 29: The Unveiling

R EVELATION IN A SINLESS WORLD

In the twilight of John's long life, when his hair shone white as lamb's wool and his eyes reflected the depth of eternity, he was taken to a high mountain in the Spirit. There, the veil between the visible and the eternal was lifted—not to reveal destruction, but **glory**, not judgment upon sin, but the **fullness of the Kingdom**.

The scroll he received, known now as **The Unveiling**, was not a prophecy of calamity, but of **completion**. It was the final song in the grand symphony of God's Edenic creation—a vision of **oneness**, **worship**, and **everlasting light**.

THE SEVEN VOICES OF THE SPIRIT

John beheld seven blazing torches before the throne—the fullness of the Spirit—each torch singing with a different voice:

1. **The Voice of Wisdom**, echoing the cries of the prophets fulfilled.
2. **The Voice of Peace**, proclaiming rest to every corner of creation.
3. **The Voice of Praise**, from every nation, tribe, and tongue.
4. **The Voice of Memory**, recalling the deeds of love throughout history.
5. **The Voice of Unity**, binding all in one accord.
6. **The Voice of Hope**, speaking of tomorrow's wonders.
7. **The Voice of God's Presence**, still and mighty, like a river of light.

John fell to his knees, and One stood before him—radiant, ageless, and clothed in linen like lightning.

"I am the Alpha and the Omega," said the Anointed, "who is, and who was, and who is to come—the Everlasting." – Revelations 1:8

THE LAMB UPON THE THRONE

John beheld a vision of the throne room, not as a courtroom of judgment, but as a **cathedral of joy**.

At the center stood a Lamb—not slain, but **crowned**, not broken, but **robed in majesty**. Around Him, the twenty-four elders danced, casting their crowns in jubilation.

"Worthy is the Lamb who dwells among us," they sang, **"for through Him, all was restored, and in Him, all is fulfilled."** – Revelations 5:12 (Revised for Eternal Eden)

And from every corner of Eden, from the rivers of Zion to the Isles of the Far Light, the people joined in chorus:

"To Him who sits on the throne and to the Lamb be blessing and honor and glory and might forever and ever!" – Revelations 5:13

THE BOOK OF THE LIVING

The Lamb held a scroll—not sealed, but open. It was the **Book of the Living**, written with the names of every soul who had walked in God's way since the beginning. In a sinless world, there was no fear of exclusion. The book sang the story of **each life**, a tapestry of holy moments, sacred work, and divine fellowship.

Children rejoiced to hear their names spoken from the book, and elders wept with joy to see the stories of their ancestors retold with light.

A NEW HEAVEN, A NEW EARTH

John saw the fullness of Eden—the **Heavenly City descending**, not because the old was broken, but because the time had come for **eternal union**.

The New Jerusalem sparkled like crystal jasper, adorned with gardens, rivers, temples of song, and streets that echoed the footsteps of angels and saints.

"Behold," spoke the Eternal Voice, **"the dwelling of God is with His people, and they shall see His face."** – Revelations 21:3 (Revised for Eternal Eden)

There was no temple there, for **the Lamb was the temple**. No sun, for **the Glory of God was the light**, and no night, for **the Spirit illumined all**.

THE RIVER AND THE TREE

At the heart of the city, the River of Life flowed, clear as morning rain. On either side grew the **Tree of Life**, bearing twelve kinds of fruit, one for each tribe and nation. Its leaves shimmered like emerald, and the people gathered beneath it to sing, learn, and share.

"The leaves of the tree are for the celebration of the nations," John wrote, **"and its fruit gives joy everlasting."** – Revelations 22:2 (Revised for Eternal Een)

THE BRIDE AND THE INVITATION

The people of Eden, united as one, were called **the Bride**, and the Lamb rejoiced in them as a groom rejoices in his beloved.

"Come," said the Spirit and the Bride. **"Come, all who thirst. Drink freely from the waters of life."**

The invitation echoed across all creation—not as a call to escape sin, but as a celebration of **communion with the Holy One**.

THE FINAL WORD

John, heart full and spirit overwhelmed, closed the scroll with tears of joy.

"He who testifies to these things says, 'Yes, I am coming soon.'
Amen. Come, Lord Jesus.
The grace of the Lord be with all. Amen." – Revelations 22:20 (Revised for Eternal Eden)

With that, the Eternal Scroll was sealed—not as an ending, but as **a beginning without end**.

Chapter 30: The Everlasting Eden

A WORLD WITHOUT END

The Purpose of This Scroll

This book is not a rewriting of Scripture, nor a replacement for the Holy Bible. It is a **sacred imagining**, a faithful exploration of what might have been—**a world untouched by sin**, where the fullness of God's intention is seen, known, and lived.

From the beginning, the Scriptures have told the story of both human frailty and divine redemption. But what if the story had never required redemption at all? What if Lucifer had not rebelled? What if Adam and Eve had never tasted the fruit? What if humankind had walked, uninterrupted, in the **glory of the Garden**?

This scroll—the vision you now hold—is born from **that sacred question**:
What if the world knew no sin?

Though sin has always existed in the fallen record of Earth, it was not part of God's heart for us. It was not the intention. Before there was rebellion, there was **fellowship**. Before exile, **Eden**. This book dares to dream of a creation **unfractured**, a humanity **untainted**, and a Kingdom **unshaken**.

And now, as the final words are written, we return to that dream—not as fantasy, but as a vision of the **very real future** promised by God: a return to His original plan. A forever Eden.

A new heaven and new earth where **the Lamb walks among His people** and where **all is as it should have been.**

Life in the Everlasting Eden

In the world that now is—the **Everlasting Eden**—there is no temple, for **God Himself is the dwelling place**. No veil separates the people from His presence. The light of the sun is surpassed by the radiance of the Lamb, and the song of creation rises unceasingly in every corner of the earth made new.

The Tree of Life grows again, **its branches stretching over the river of crystal**, its leaves shimmering with joy and wisdom. Children play beneath its shade, listening to the stories of the ancients—of Adam and Eve, of David and Solomon, of Esther, Ruth, and Paul—not as tales of loss and rescue, but as *songs of fulfilled purpose*.

Time is no longer an enemy. There is no aging, no decay. The passage of seasons are not marked by sorrow, but by **wonders**; flowers that bloom in praise, stars that dance in worship, creatures that sing in harmony with the heart of their Creator.

Relationships Redeemed

Love in Eden is **pure and eternal**. Husbands and wives walk together as one, not needing healing or forgiveness, for their hearts are whole and filled only with goodness. Parents teach their children the ways of the Lord without fear, without tears, guiding them in joy and delight.

Communities gather daily—not in need, but in celebration. There is no competition, no comparison, no jealousy. Each soul shines uniquely, fully alive in their God-given purpose, and yet perfectly united with all others in a **divine harmony** that cannot be broken.

Creativity Unleashed

In this Kingdom, **creativity flows like rivers**. Artists paint the glory of God across endless canvases of sky and sea. Writers compose scrolls of wisdom and beauty. Musicians sing songs that echo the very heartbeat of the Spirit. Builders design cities of light. Inventors create not out of necessity, but out of joy, for there is no brokenness to mend—only beauty to uncover.

Science explores the mysteries of God's creation not to control, but to *wonder*. Math is the language of design, music the rhythm of thought, and language the gift of sharing love in endless nuance.

Worship Without Ceasing

Worship is not an event—it is the breath of Eden. Every step, every word, every moment is **a sacred act**. People worship while they plant gardens, care for animals, or share meals. Songs rise in fields, in mountains, in valleys, in cities of radiant stone.

The saints of every age gather to sing Psalms beside David. Isaiah walks the hills with the faithful, reciting his visions aloud. Peter teaches alongside Paul, not sermons of sin and rescue, but **truths of glory and growth**.

The angels still sing, but now their harmonies are joined by countless voices from every nation and tribe, whose song is not one of salvation—but of **completion**.

Learning Forever

Knowledge never ends in the Everlasting Eden. With no pride, no envy, no forgetfulness, every soul is **forever learning**—not from books alone, but from walking with God Himself.

Jesus sits with young and old alike, teaching the mysteries of the stars, the meaning of parables, and the depth of the Father's love. The Spirit whispers wisdom through the wind, and the Father is near, always near, not in wrath or distance, but in **delight**.

Prophets continue to speak—not of warnings, but of *wonders*. Teachers lead not toward repentance, but toward deeper awe. And every generation adds to the eternal scroll—a story with no end.

The Kingdom Without End

This Kingdom is not just for Earth, but for the **universe reborn**. The galaxies shine with purpose. Time is not a prison. The saints explore without fear. They journey through space and spirit, never alone, always with one another and with God.

There are no gates in the New Jerusalem—for there is no danger. The rivers flow without pollution. The animals roam without harm. The lion and the lamb lie down together still—not as a miracle, but as a certainty.

And at the center of it all—the Throne. From it flows light, laughter, love. Around it gather all who ever lived in harmony with God's design. And above it shines the Word made flesh, now dwelling forever with His people.

And so we return to Eden.
Not with sorrow or scars, but in celebration.
Not because we were rescued, but because we were always meant to be here.
The Garden never closed. It only waited.

This is the **world without sin**—
the **world as God intended**—
the **Everlasting Eden**.

www.ingramcontent.com/pod-product-compliance
Lightning Source LLC
Chambersburg PA
CBHW070621120726